Best Wishes
from
Jenny Chaplin

# A Life to Live in Glasgow

## Jenny Telfer Chaplin

BeWrite Books

Published internationally by BeWrite Books, UK.
32 Bryn Road South, Wigan, Lancashire, WN4 8QR.



A CIP catalogue record for this book is available from the British Library

ISBN: 978-1-905202-58-4

Also available in eBook format.

Produced by BeWrite Books
www.bewrite.net

Jenny Chaplin is well known to loyal readers worldwide for her books on Scottish social history and for her articles in the *Scots Magazine* and the *Scottish Banner.*

As a Fellow of the Society of Antiquaries of Scotland, Jenny is well qualified to write her historical novels after years of research into and writing about Scottish social history.

She now writes her novels in her centuries old cottage on the Island of Bute under the name Jenny Telfer Chaplin to differentiate between her fiction and non-fiction writing.

**Also by Jenny Telfer Chaplin:**
The Kinnons of Candleriggs
The Widow of Candleriggs
The Ashes of Candleriggs

# A Life to Live in Glasgow

# Part 1

## Chapter 1

### *1 July 1899*

The early morning light filtered through the threadbare curtains at the window of the tenement flat but for all the joy it brought the three young women in the room at the dawning of a summer's day, it might as well have been the dark of mid-winter. Engaged as they were in this most secret of tasks, the darkness was already in their souls. As one tear-stained, matted-haired woman writhed in agony on the bed, the second with her untrained, so-called midwifery skills, struggled to bring into the world a reluctant baby, and the third member of their conspiracy sat continuously chewing her fingernails to the quick as if already doubting the wisdom of their actions.

As they all knew the pregnant woman had been in the throes of her tortuous labour for what seemed to them an endless age but which was in reality a little more than ten hours. Despite the midwife's well-meaning but feeble efforts the baby was no nearer to making his or her way into the waiting world. The constant urging to keep pushing but to do so quietly lest her screams be heard by the bairns across the landing in the neighbour's flat did even less to comfort the patient than the regular mopping of her brow with a vinegar-soaked rag.

With the light gaining strength the appointments of the room gradually became clearer – the black steel sink under the window;

the goose-necked cold water tap; the wax-cloth-covered table; the mantelpiece with its regulation pair of wally dugs, brass candlesticks, tea caddy, and overhanging gas mantle; the crammed to capacity pulley with its array of vests, towels, nappies, and knickers; the home-made wee creepie stool; the rather decrepit armchair into which the 'Heid o' the Hoose' would slump when home between stints as an ocean going deckhand.

Just as the rays of the sun reached the recess bed and the pain-wracked face of the young woman, with a final scream and arching of her body, she finally expelled the burden she had carried with her for nine long, weary months. What a hated burden it had been for both her and her sister. For the final months and weeks of her pregnancy Meg had ventured out only at night enveloped in an enormous, moth-eaten shawl, while her sister, Nellie, had waddled round the streets of Bridgeton and her already child-filled tenement home with a cushion tied to her waist creating the supposed bump of a growing baby in her belly.

The self-styled midwife cleaned up the baby, wrapped it in a crocheted shawl, and held out the latest bundle of humanity.

"There she is then, a bonnie wee baby."

When there was no reply, nor even as much as answering smiles from her audience, Hannah persisted. "Weel, if naethin else, surely between the pair o ye wi aw the fine planning ye've done, surely tae God ye've at least thought up a name for the puir wee bastard."

As the harshness and bitter reality of this hated word sounded in the stillness of the early morning somehow its echoes seemed to hang in the air between them. Finally Nellie got slowly to her feet and glaring at Hannah said in a voice low with menace: "Bastard? Naethin o the kind. Don't you iver again use that hideous word referring to that poor wee mite."

Hannah nodded and opened her mouth as if to speak, but Nellie hadn't finished with her tirade.

"See her? See that wee scrap o humanity – you can call her any first name ye like, but Ah'm tellin ye this: as far as her surname goes … she'll bear ma husband's name, jist like aw the rest of ma ither bairns. Dae ye understand?" Hannah nodded. "Jist in case ye don't get the picture, frae this minute on ye keep your silence – silent as the grave would jist aboot dae it."

Hannah locked glances with the red-faced Mrs Nellie Bryden then slowly and deliberately rolled down her sleeves.

"Oh aye! That's one thing sure … Ah'll no be saying a word tae naebody. Apart frae onythin else – and maybe ye dinnae ken *this,* Mrs Know-it-all, but see the very minute ye gie false details aboot an illegitimate bairn on any official document, like it or lump it, ye will be breaking the law o the land, so ye will."

From the quick indrawn breath and the look on Nellie's face Hannah grinned, taking it that her barb had struck home and this was indeed news to Nellie.

"For all Ah ken the pair o youse might weel end up in jail. So hae nae fear. Ah wouldnae want tae join ye. Frae this day forrad ma lips is sealed."

Having completed her task to her own satisfaction, the self-righteous Hannah turned and called back from the doorway: "As far as a Christian name goes, why don't ye call her Becky? Ah had an auld Aunt Becky and see her, talk aboot being lucky! Aye! She was that lucky in everythin she touched in this life that folk used tae say o her that if she fell in the Clyde she'd come up wi a gold watch. Aye! The name Becky should dae that puir faitherless bairn jist fine. For let's face it, if anybody ever needed a bit o luck in this life ye can take it frae me it's gonnae be that puir wee innocent bastard."

With the noise of the slammed door still ringing in their ears Nellie and Meg looked at each other and almost in unison said: "Right! Becky Bryden it is."

Nellie bustled around the kitchen preparing a pot of tea and said: "Right, Meg, one way and another, between the pair o us, we've battled our way through this bit o bother jist fine and dandy."

A wan-faced Meg nodded and, exhausted, fell back. The pain

and trauma of the night faded and she slipped into a dreamlike state …

Alex Cartside was so much more sophisticated than anyone Meg had ever met before. His polished manners and refined speech attracted her right from the very first time she saw him standing at the podium lecturing the class on the finer points of diction – "So necessary for a teacher to give a good example to her pupils."

She was thrilled when in the second week he had complimented her in front of the whole class on her excellent speech and speaking voice. Their accidental meeting in Miss Cranston's on Sauchiehall Street was the high point of the third week at the Normal School and she readily agreed to his proposal that they meet at Kelvingrove Art Gallery. There, he said, he could expand her horizon, discussing with her the excellent art, and thus making her a better teacher.

The visit to the gallery was very pleasant and at the afternoon tea which naturally followed Meg was charmed and readily agreed to further meetings.

Miss Euphemia Edgar, the spinster teacher who had taken Meg in when her parents died and with whom she still lived, warned her against 'any romantic entanglement' which would end her career in teaching. Meg had laughed. Alex was a lecturer at the Normal School, a good ten years older than she; he was simply good-heartedly interested in helping her become a better teacher.

However, as the meetings went on Meg was aware that while still formal and proper Alex now occasionally held her hand and once daringly put his arm round her waist. The first kiss in the twilight walking in Kelvingrove Park startled but thrilled her and she found herself kissing him back. Meg declined the next invitation, but Alex had pulled her aside after class and apologised, saying he had been carried away by the moment and that it wouldn't happen again. Their next meeting was again formal but in subsequent meetings they moved to amorous caresses and before Meg stopped to think they were in his rooms and it was too late to think.

In mid-November she discovered she was pregnant. Alex's response to the news shocked her. He implied that she, a woman of loose morals, couldn't possibly be sure the baby was his, and that anyway he was moving back in with his wife from whom he had had a temporary separation. He was resigning his post at the Normal School and taking up a similar post in Canada in the New Year.

Meg left Miss Edgar's comfortable home saying her older sister needed her and she moved in with Nellie.

Later that day after copious amounts of tea Nellie sighed.

"Why on earth ye had tae gie everythin away like that, it fair beats me. Honest tae God the mair Ah think aboot it, the angrier and mair het-up Ah get. Tae think o aw the chances *ye* had that Ah niver even got a look at … ye were clever; ye got tae stay on at school efter Maw and Paw died and that dried up auld spinster o an English teacher wi the posh talk and stuff took ye in. Ye even got tae begin yer training for tae be a schoolteacher. A schoolteacher by God – and then …"

Meg eased herself up on the bed and reached out a detaining hand.

"Och, Nellie, don't. Please don't go on and on about it."

Nellie brushed Meg's hand aside and shouted: "Och, Nellie, nothin. This is somethin Ah hae tae say and God help me Ah *will* say it. It makes me fair boil wi rage when Ah think how bloody stupid ye've been. Where were aw yer brilliant brains then when ye were daeing the business wi him? Was aw yer high intellect and yer high-falutin manners doon therr skeeterin aboot in yer knickers?"

Meg's face became even paler and she gasped.

Seeing the effect of her diatribe on her sister, Nellie relented somewhat.

"Och, listen, hen, what's done cannae be undone but wi yer

lover by noo over the seas tae the colonies tae escape his responsibilities, God alone knows what on earth ye'll dae noo. But one thing Ah dae ken. Ye'll no be able tae stay here in ma hoose. Ma ain tribe o bairns will be back frae across the landing the morn's morn and Ah'll need tae introduce them tae their new wee sister Becky. Apart frae onythin else ma man could be arriving back frae the high seas any day noo. He's gonnae be surprised enough tae see another new bairn – although mind you the way he went on at the hochmagandie on his last leave it shouldnae be as big a surprise."

Meg blushed at her sister's use of the coarse old Scotch word for intercourse. "It was fortunate that this trip took him away for just over the nine months."

Nellie snorted. "Rab will deal aw right wi another mewlin wean, but the one thing he couldnae stomach is your fancy Kelvinside speechifyin, yer prissy manners, and yer high-falutin ideas. Naw, naw. Rab jist couldnae deal wi a high and mighty lady o quality such as ye've turned intae over the years. So ye'd better start thinkin aboot where it is ye're gonna be livin, since ye cannae see yersel back wi yer teacher freen, and ye havenae the ghost o an idea as tae whit ye're gonnae dae tae earn an honest crust."

# Chapter 2

Nellie's words sank into Meg's already sore, troubled brain. For the rest of that memorable day and far into the night, as Meg tossed on a sleepless pillow, the words kept on hammering their relentless message at her.

Early next morning Meg barely had time to sip at the cup of hot, sweet tea Nellie handed her before Nellie said: "Well? Reached any decisions yet? At least ye've had time to sleep on it …"

"Sleep on it! Sleep on it did you say, Nellie? With all this on my mind?"

Nellie waved her sister's words aside with a dismissive gesture. "Hmph! Ye've probably had a hell of a lot more sleep that me. Ah wis up and doon the hale night attendin tae that mewlin brat o yers."

Meg bridled. "Her name is Becky, if you don't mind, not mewling brat."

"Listen, hen, Ah don't give a damn whit her bloody name is, but whit Ah dae care aboot is this … ma man Rab could come roisterin back frae the high seas ony day noo. Ye'll hae tae be weel clear o ma hoose before then. Surely ye can understaun that?"

Meg sighed. "I know, I know, so you don't need to keep harping on about it. As to my own instincts … I'd love to stay on here with wee Becky, but I know I can't. It's impossible."

"Impossible is right. At least that's somethin we can baith agree on. Too bloody right it's impossible. Right, noo we've settled that, what exactly is it that ye're plannin tae dae for tae keep yer ain body and soul together? No tae mention haein the means tae go slippin me the odd half-croon backhander for looking efter yer wee b… er for feedin and clothin yer wee Becky."

Silence greeted this and Nellie went on: "Ye'll need tae get a job o some kind and the good God above alone kens whit that will be. For there's one thing for certain sure, ye've certainly buggered up yer chance o iver reachin the giddy heights of social superiority o being a schoolma'am."

"Nellie, would you please, please stop going on about my lost chances? If anyone on this planet earth is aware of what a horrendous mess I've made of my life it is me. When I think of how easily men can wriggle out of their paternal responsibilities I could weep from now till Kingdom Come."

"Aye, ye were right stupid aboot that scunnersome lout that left you to fend for yersel with a bun in yer oven. Ah've been lucky wi ma Rab. He works his fingers tae the bone slavin away on the high seas on that boat jist tae feed and clothe oor squad o weans. Never a cross word passes his lips even if every time he gets back Ah've got another new bairn waitin for tae greet its faither. Aye, one mair mouth tae feed disnae bother him, and ye can thank yer lucky stars for it, otherwise Ah'd no hae been able for tae take wee Becky aff your hands. Aye, a man among men, that's ma guid man Rab."

Meg pressed her lips together for the sake of peace as she thought of *her* picture of Rab – a drunken, womanising, controlling man; the seafarer home from the sea with money in his pocket and 'rarin to go' on his usual jaunts to the many houffs and pubs of the City of Glasgow.

After a short silence Nellie shook herself. "There's ower much tae dae this morn for tae stand here bletherin. Whit in God's name kinda job dae ye hope tae get?"

Meg frowned and chewed her lip then quite suddenly her face cleared.

"I think I *may* just have stumbled on an answer."

Nellie stared at her sister, a look of disbelief on her face. "Ye really think that woman would gie ye a job? Why on earth would she? Let's face it hen ye've nae experience nor qualifications for tae work in a haberdashery, or any other dashery for that matter."

Meg gave a rueful smile. "If we're being totally honest I'm not qualified for anything at all now, am I? But the thing is, Miss Martin, the elderly lady who owns it, she and I struck up quite a rapport when I used to buy some oddments in her shop while I was at the college in Dundas Vale."

Nellie rolled her eyes to heaven. "Listen, hen, Ah don't care what it was that ye struck up the auld biddy, but Ah still don't see why in God's name she would gie ye a job. She's no yer fairy godmother nor naethin is she?"

Meg waved aside her sister's words. "I became quite friendly with Miss Martin. I think she just needed someone to talk to. She used to tell me about her old mother and –"

Nellie snorted. "Fascinatin stuff!"

Ignoring her sister's sarcasm, Meg went on: "Anyway be that as it may, the point is she once said, since I had a lovely speaking voice and compassionate manner, if ever I found teaching a class of unruly children was not to my liking she would be more than happy to give me a job. So there you have it! I've made up my mind. I'll go and see her."

"Right, Meg. For the love o God dae it sooner rather than later afore the auld biddy changes her mind. Eh no?"

# Chapter 3

Miss Petronella Martin was absolutely delighted with her new assistant. Not only did the desperate-for-paid-work Meg Spence treat her employer with the respect and deference due to an astute business woman of the social calibre of Petronella Martin, Meg with her careful vowels, absence of the Glasgow glottal stop, neat appearance, and pleasant manner also charmed the customers which was excellent for repeat trade.

However, there was one thing on which they could not see eye to eye and this morning Miss Martin in a quiet spell between customers launched yet again on her favourite topic.

"I'm only saying it for you own good, my dear Meg. It just isn't natural, or even healthy, for a lovely young woman like you, with all the proper social graces, to spend all of her free time cooped up in that one room in your boarding house. You really do need to get out more. Go places, do things, meet people of your own age and social position. Perhaps even be introduced to some eligible young bachelors of good social and financial standing. Do face the facts, my dear Meg; you surely don't want to end up like me, a spinster of the Parish, with neither husband nor child to call my own."

*If Miss Martin ever met Nellie and her coarse speech and manners what on earth would she think? Oh My Lord, if she ever found out about Becky I'd be out of a job quicker than a flash. And as for meeting eligible young bachelors ... well ... my one adventure was, as it turned out, neither eligible nor a bachelor. I don't think I'm ready to try that again for now.*

"Are you all right, my dear?" Miss Martin peered at Meg, inches from her face, and placed a hand on her shoulder.

"Oh, yes, sorry, Miss Martin. I was miles away. But yes, I did hear what you were saying. You think I should get out more – escape from time to time from the confines of my poky little room."

Miss Martin sat back and nodded. "So you *were* listening after all. Well now, about that room in your boarding house … I've been meaning to talk to you about that. Recently I've been giving a lot of thought to your living conditions. A room in a boarding house with who knows what unsavoury characters to be met at the common meal table is not really suitable. Here is what I've come up with … just an idea, of course … but one which I think could well be of interest to you and advantageous both financially and socially. So let's have our morning tea and I'll explain matters to you in detail."

# Chapter 4

It had been a long, tiring, and indeed rather stressful day at the haberdashery … and not least on account of Miss Martin's detailed outlining of her so-called master plan to have Meg leave her 'socially unsuitable' accommodation and take a room at Miss Martin's home.

On Meg's way back to her lodgings her employer's words were still ringing through her head as she mentally considered the advantages and, yes, the very real possible disadvantages of such a move, involving, as it would, helping with the care of Miss Martin's elderly mother. The more she thought about it the more Meg was inclined to accept the kind offer even with the strings attached.

*Yes*, Meg thought. *In many ways it would suit me very well. But there's no need to make up my mind for a while yet. After all, once I commit myself to such a scheme that's me locked in.*

As Meg quickened her steps along the darkening city streets she thought: *Strange that remark Miss Martin made about my meeting up with unsavoury characters at the lodging house.*

The elderly spinster was more accurate than she might have guessed. It wasn't only at the communal dining-table there was danger from unwelcome advances. It would not be the first time that Meg had been harassed and ogled by another tenant in an upper hallway. Even in the street on her way from work she had been accosted by men appearing from otherwise deserted alleyways.

In allowing her thoughts to dwell on this troublesome aspect of her daily life, Meg felt she was in danger of losing the meagre self-confidence she had managed to dredge up after the debacle of her fall from grace and the horrendous trauma of having given birth to an illegitimate child. Perhaps what her sister Nellie had said, in her usual less than ladylike language, that as a 'fallen woman' she was indeed sending out the wrong signals to, "randy, gaspin for it, dirty auld men."

Meg was unsure what these real or imagined signals could be. *However, being a lone, unaccompanied, obviously unattached, yet fairly presentable young woman living in a lodging house that was perhaps giving out an unintentional come hither look. Of course, those were the wrong signals the never ending stream of commercial travellers and other such casuals who passed through the rooming-house thought she was sending.*

That night at the evening meal while firmly ignoring the lustful stares of her known tormentors Meg instead listened politely to the conversation of the new arrival across the table from her.

He proved to be a most interesting dinner companion with tales of his travels and amusing anecdotes. Alone at the table when the others had left, he bashfully and with boyish naivety confessed: "I'm a lay preacher. I don't generally let this fact be known to casual acquaintances. I suppose I fear that because I've found God it makes me, in some people's eyes, a sort of latter day goody-goody mama's boy."

Meg and her new-found friend laughed at this and Meg, feeling herself to be on safe grounds with this sound, upright citizen, light-heartedly said: "Don't worry, Mr Lay Preacher, sir, you're dastardly secret is safe with me."

On that happy note Meg headed upstairs to soak her feet, aching after a long day standing in the shop, then to unpin and brush out her hair. Finally she sought the comfort of her single bed in the cell-like freezing room she now called home.

Almost asleep, something brought her fully awake and she sat up in bed to peer round the room in the faint light afforded by the street's flickering gas lamp outside her window. There it was again. A sound she couldn't quite place.

*A mouse? Oh Lord, don't let it be a mouse.*

Meg pulled the patchwork cover tight around her and over her head and lying down again tried to get back to sleep. The sound came again, but this time Meg, now fully awake, identified it. No mouse was big enough or clever enough to be trying to turn the key in her bedroom door. While she considered herself a coward, a shivering wreck of a woman when faced with a mouse she would be damned if any lustful man would ever again ruin her life. Meg, as she rose, was just in time to see a sheet of paper being slid through the wide gap under her door.

*This is no secret love letter,* she thought. *Any minute now my bedroom door key is going to be pushed from the lock to fall onto that paper and be slid back under the door into the grasping hand of whoever is there.*

She took hold of the key and quietly removed it from the lock. That done, she looked round the room for anything of sufficient weight with which to barricade her door. The rickety old chair certainly wouldn't fit the bill nor would the wobbly cane bedside table. If she could possibly drag over the solid oak chest of drawers, however, that would do the trick. Using every ounce of her strength she dragged the piece of furniture towards the door. Before the chest was finally in place, with her bare foot she pushed the offending piece of paper under the door and back to its owner. With one last surge of energy the chest with a final thump was firmly in place. That achieved, a stream of the most vile, foul language was directed at Meg from the unseen, would-be lecher.

Even with the security of the physical barrier Meg's mental torture of what might have happened went on well into the early hours of the morning. To add to her distress her tormentor was apparently in the room next to hers with his bed seemingly on the other side of the paper-thin wall between them. Throughout the rest of Meg's terror-filled night he banged, knocked, and scratched on the dividing wall to the accompaniment of drunken shouts about: "… the f***ing whore who led a poor fellow on with her bedroom eyes … then got cold feet when a fellow followed up on her invitation."

When Meg came down for breakfast next morning it was all she could do not to gag at the very thought of eating the porridge Mrs Farley set before her. However, feeling somehow ashamed and dirty as if the night's escapade had indeed been an unlooked for and certainly unwelcome result of her 'bedroom eyes', Meg was determined to act as normally as possible and not let pass even a hint of what had happened. When Mrs Farley brought in the sparsely filled rack of toast Meg noticed that for once she seemed to be dining alone.

Almost as if she had caught Meg's unspoken thought Mrs Farley leaned forward and said: "It's a pity you weren't down quicker. You've just missed that handsome new lodger of ours. You both seemed to be getting along so well at supper last night … quite taken with you he was."

Meg's head jerked up from her contemplation of the toast and the two small regulation curly knobs of butter.

"Oh, now don't you go imagining romance where none existed, Mrs Farley. I was merely being polite and sociable that was all. He's a lay preacher no less."

Mrs Farley nodded absently. "Well, that's as may be. Anyway, ships that pass in the night. To tell you the truth, dear, I very nearly missed him myself. You know how deaf I am. He had one foot out the door when I came through. He said he hadn't wanted to disturb me at such an early hour especially since he wasn't hungry and didn't want anything to eat. Something about a business meeting at the Trongate. All a bit of a rush and he wouldn't after all be spending another night with us. He's going to collect his little attaché case later today and would pay me then for both nights anyway. Isn't that really generous of him? Such a nice man, don't you think?"

Meg gave a noncommittal ghost of a smile and thought: *Unless I'm very much mistaken, Mrs Farley, we have both seen the last of that handsome new lodger, lay preacher or not.*

On her way to work half an hour later Meg mused that the 'ship that had passed in the night' while cheating the besotted, stone-deaf Mrs Farley out of her money had at least done some good. His fumbled efforts at intended rape had decided Meg on her plan of actions. She would accept Petronella Martin's offer to move into her Great Western Road home and help out with Mrs Martin's elderly mother.

*Yes, indeed. What could be better? Yes, something good had certainly come out of something bad.*

# Chapter 5

Each time Meg went to her sister's home to see wee baby Becky, inevitably she came away feeling both delighted and downcast. She was always charmed and re-assured to see how wonderfully well the baby was progressing in Nellie's care, but she despaired at the fleeting quality of her visits and the gnawing certainty that her own darling wee Becky would never in this life be able to acknowledge her true birth mother.

On this particular evening she was aware of an ever-growing feeling of resentment gathering strength like a cancer within her very soul. She was still mentally raw after her narrow escape from the lecherous lodger as a result of which she was now on the verge of moving to Miss Martin's house, and Nellie's news tonight made her feel as if her entire world was collapsing round her.

As she made her way back to her lodgings along Bridgeton's bustling Main Street Meg replayed in her mind that night's visit …

"Well," Nellie said, "it's mibbe jist as well ye'll soon be stravaigin across the Clyde tae Great Western Road –"

Thinking Nellie was referring, however obliquely, yet again, to her 'airs and graces' and meaning that in such a house Meg would be well suited to the more rarefied, toffee-nosed area of the City of Glasgow Meg started to protest, but Nellie pressed on.

"Uch, for hivven's sake, Meg. Therr's a helluva lot mair tae life than aw such bloody falderals. Guid God Almighty, if anybody on this earth should ken that surely to hivven it's ye, ye daft bitch."

When Meg insisted she still didn't know what Nellie was trying to tell her, Nellie shooed her brood of children into the hall out of earshot and said: "Uch, ye're supposed tae be the brainy one o the family. Ah've telt ye once but Ah'll tell ye again … it's ma guid man, Rab. He's fed up wi yon lang sea voyages and bloody months on end without sae much as a sniff o the marriage bed. That's whit for Ah telt ye he's got himsel a job on the boats that gae up and doon the Clyde atween the Broomielaw and the likes o Dunoon and Rothesay."

Meg realised with a pang that Rab's totally unexpected career change very effectively put paid to her frequent visits as she remembered Nellie's previous words on Rab's feelings towards herself.

"Not only will ye be seeing less o Wee Becky, but ye'll need tae be payin me a wheen mair … at least another couple of hauf croons a week should jist aboot dae it."

Hearing Meg's intake of breath at this news Nellie went on: "Think on it, hen. Rab'll no be gettin sich guid wages for yon skittery wee trips up and doon the Clyde. Onywey, if yer no gonnae be forkin oot a king's ransom for lodgins, ye'll be able to gie me mair o yer hard-earned sillar tae keep Becky fed and clothed in ma hoose."

# Chapter 6

Towards the end of that same week Meg said farewell to Mrs Farley and later said a tight-lipped hello to old Mrs Martin.

Despite the fact that the main rooms in the house were high-ceilinged and spacious, the room allocated to Meg proved to be neither and resembled nothing so much as a nun's cubicle or a prisoner's cell.

Meg smiled grimly. *Perhaps both descriptions are very apt for not only will I be living like a nun in this mausoleum, but I'll be a prisoner and a slave to the demands, whims, and fancies of that cantankerous old woman. Oh well, as the saying goes I've made my bed, so now I'll just have to lie on it.*

One consolation was that she still greatly enjoyed her work in the haberdashery and she knew that in Petronella's eyes she was a Godsend as in addition to working hard in the shop Meg also gave of her best to old Mrs Martin.

Days, weeks, and months drifted past with fewer and fewer opportunities to visit her daughter Becky and in a quiet spell in the shop Meg was thinking sadly about this as she tidied up a box of ribbons. Head bent to her task Meg heard a sound from across the counter and looking up was astonished to find herself eyeball to eyeball with a beshawled Nellie. Wonder of wonders there was Becky wrapped up cosily in the shawl. At first too surprised at this unexpected encounter to think or speak rationally Meg could only stare in delighted amazement at her visitors.

Nellie finally said: "Don't worry yer heid, hen. Ah'm no here looking for mair money, for gie ye yer due, Meg, yer postal orders aye arrive regular as clockwork."

Meg nodded, but wondered then why her sister had chosen to come to the shop.

Before she could ask, Nellie forestalled her. "Ah happened tae bump intae yer auld landlady and she let the cat oot o the bag as tae where ye worked. So, Ah thocht tae masel there's nae time like the present and jist hopped ontae a tramcaur, and here Ah am."

Since it would be clear to the most casual observer the shawlie woman was not in the process of buying anything and was taking an inordinate amount of time chatting in her loud coarse voice Meg was aware that Miss Martin was casting meaningful glances in her direction. Even so, Meg, greatly daring, stretched out a trembling hand to caress the sweet little baby face peering out from the folds of the shawl.

Miss Martin materialised at Meg's side and in her most carefully articulated, down-putting voice said: "Is there something with which we may help Modom?"

Nellie glared at Meg and gave a mocking tilt of her head towards Miss Martin, clearly waiting for Meg to introduce her. The uneasy silence stretched and the moment of opportunity passed. Drawing herself to her full height, Nellie assumed her best attempt at 'proper, pan-loaf speech' and said: "No, thank ye, my good woman, there's absolutely nothing here in yer little shop for me. I think I'll try some of the better stores in Sauchiehall Street. Good day to ye."

With that and a 'more in sorrow than in anger' look at Meg, Nellie, her head held high and cuddling the precious bundle of Becky, marched out of the haberdashery.

Petronella pursed her lips as the door pinged shut behind Nellie and turning to Meg said: "Honestly! Some people. Sauchiehall Street indeed. Paddy's Market would be rather more to her taste … if her speech and that flea-bitten shawl are anything to go by. I can't think why the likes of her and her snivelling child bothered to come in to my lovely haberdashery in the first place, can you Meg?"

When Meg's only reply was a sorrowful shake of the head, Petronella wiped her hands in a grand theatrical manner as if dismissing the recent representative of the lower orders. She turned to Meg with a smile. "Now, what about a cup of tea in the back shop? We could both do with a reviver, don't you think? We'll leave young Cissie in charge for half-an-hour. It's high time she was taking more responsibility. Anyway, there's something I want to discuss with you in private."

Over the tea Petronella's private matter was her hobby horse about Meg's social life or rather the lack of it. "There's another soirée coming soon at the church hall and I'm determined *you will go* this time. I've seen the way that young man Jack Dunn looks at you in church since you met him at the last soirée I managed to get you to attend."

# Chapter 7

Wee Becky was now a little over a year old and a bonnier baby was not to be seen in the whole of Glasgow. Although kept busy with her work at the haberdashery and helping to look after Mrs Martin, Meg managed to visit her child as often as possible and whenever Rab's absence at work presented an opportunity she took advantage of it. On these occasions she marvelled at her baby's progress and thanked Nellie for all her help.

However, on one evening in the late summer of 1900 as the two sisters sat together over a pot of tea, with Nellie's own children playing round their feet while Becky slept peacefully, Meg wore a worried frown.

Observing this for some time Nellie finally said: "Listen, Meg. For the love o the wee man will ye just stop worryin about nothin? What'll happen will happen and there's naethin the likes o us can do about it."

"Don't worry! Don't worry," Meg snapped. "Hmph. That's easily said. Do you even know what I've been talking about? For heaven's sake, Nellie, do you pay attention to nothing that's going on?"

Nellie glowered. "That's bluidy charmin, I must say, especially comin from the likes o ye. Oh, Ah pey attention aw right … damn sure Ah dae. Ah spend every wakin hour takin care o a houseful of bairns – no forgettin yer ain wee bas– er, yer ain wee precious Becky. And if that disnae fit the bill o payin attention, mibbe yer ladyship wid climb doon aff yer high horse lang enough tae tell me jist whit the hell we're talking aboot."

Meg matched stare for stare with her sister before finally saying: "Nellie, can you see nothing beyond the confines of your own pathetic little world? What I am talking about, in fact, what the entire population of Glasgow – with one possible exception – is discussing is the latest outbreak of plague. The whole city is in a panic. And no wonder. Imagine! Eleven cases of bubonic plague and another ninety-three contacts under observation at Belvedere Hospital. Surely even *you* are concerned about that?"

Nellie pushed back a lock of hair which had escaped the confines of her dust-cap. Once that had been done to her entire satisfaction, only then did she deign to reply. "Oh, that? The plague – is that whit yer gettin aw worked up aboot? Uch, ye cannae believe all them facts and figures yon Sanitary Chambers is aye churnin oot. Keeps aw them pen pushers in cushy jobs, if ye ask me."

Meg pointed an admonitory finger at her sister. "Well then, I *am* asking you, aren't you the least bit concerned? Of course, you are at liberty to believe whatever you wish, but the fact remains bubonic plague is quite definitely a force to be reckoned with. The very thought of it here, rampant in Glasgow, scares me rigid."

Nellie sighed. "Aye, God help us, ye huvnae changed much. Ye were aye a worrier. A born worrier, so ye are. Even as a wee girl playin in the back court ye jist couldnae bear tae get yer hauns aw mucky. As for rakin through the middens like the rest o us ye'd rather run a mile and tak a runnin jump intae the Clyde." After a reflective pause Nellie continued: "A great worrier indeed. Jist a damn shame ye hadnae worried yersell aboot the sure-fire consequences when ye done the business wi yon fly-by-nicht so called boyfriend of yers."

Meg gasped and it was all of a minute before she could trust herself to speak. "Nellie! Please. I beg of you. Please do not start that again. It's over. Finished and done with."

Nellie glared back. "Done with ye say? Hmph that's rich. Listen ye tae me, hen, it'll niver be done with. No as long as that wee wean's arsehole looks doon. One wey and another ye've got that commitment for life. And don't ye ever forget it."

Meg's lips tightened, but rather than keep a sulky silence she decided to have it out with her sister. "Why is it, Nellie, no matter what topic we start to discuss – be it the price of coal, the minister's last sermon, or even the bubonic plague – it always comes back to my fall from grace?"

Nellie allowed herself the ghost of a smile and relented. "Aye, ye're right, hen, deid right. God alone kens how we got frae a killer disease tae ye ain wee bit o bother. Ah suppose it's because ye're aye in ma mind – Ah'll niver understand how an intelligent girl like ye could – uch, tae hell, it disnae bear talkin aboot –"

"Right then, Nellie. *Don't* talk about it. That's all I ask."

To fill the empty silence between them, Nellie got to her feet and busied herself about the kitchen, finally returning with the peace offering of a fresh pot of tea.

"Onywey, therr's one thing Ah will say. Ah'm mibbe a hell o a lot better informed aboot the plague than you seem tae think. Fine weel Ah ken aw the details, whit ye might call the nitty-gritty. The plague was first reported in Thistle Street and Rose Street. But ye can tak it frae me, roon aboot here we've naethin tae worry aboot."

Meg frowned. "Nothing! You say there's nothing to worry about? How on earth do you come to that conclusion?"

Puffed up with her own importance at her superior knowledge on the subject, Nellie obviously savoured the moment before saying: "Ah'm no arrivin nowheres, hen but Ah kin tell ye this … Ah hae it on guid authority it's aw been cleaned up – done and dusted. Aye, Swept away."

Nellie paused for dramatic effect, but before she could continue Meg said: "For heaven's sake, Nellie. No one on God's earth can simply sweep away the dreaded bubonic plague as if it were the Saturday night detritus in the common close."

Nellie gave a mirthless laugh. "Ah'm buggart if Ah ken whit yer talkin aboot noo. Meg. The fact remains – Ah ken it for God's truth – no only hae the Sanitary men disinfected the hooses in yon twa streets, but they've even cleaned oot the very middens, and wid ye believe it. They've whitewashed the landins, the stairs and the closes. Aye, whitewashed them! Wid ye credit that? So Ah'm sure, in fact Ah'm deid certain, we can noo kiss guid-bye to ony mair threat of bubonic plague here in Glesga. So ye can jist stoap frettin. The bairns will be fine."

# Chapter 8

***January 1901***

Ever since the scare about the bubonic plague, which in their case, thankfully, had come to nothing, each time Nellie had made noises about the lack of money somehow or other Meg had managed to stretch her wages to go that little bit further. However, although Nellie had never again actually demanded money for her ministrations the unspoken but very real intention was there and the matter was a constant source of worry to Meg.

*Yes,* Meg thought as she hurried to work on that late January morning. *It's never-ending. Will there come a time when I can't afford to pay the necessary amount?*

As always, what made things even harder to bear, the impossibility of ever having the luxury of being able to discuss her problems with another living soul meant the questions and worries all kept swirling around unanswered in her head.

*And,* thought Meg, *as if January isn't already my most hated month of the year it's even gloomier this year with the whole city draped in hideous black crêpe for the Old Queen's mourning. No wonder I feel so down, out of sorts, and utterly depressed. What would I give for even the tiniest ray of sunshine?*

On her entry into the haberdashery she was greeted by a sombre Miss Martin. Not only was Petronella dressed in black from head to toe, the shop was festooned in black crêpe. Every available surface from the shop's counter to the heavy brass cash-till was covered. Even the elegant chairs set out for the comfort and convenience of the customers were shrouded. As if this display was insufficient to show Miss Martin's due and proper respect for the newly-deceased Queen Victoria, on the counter itself was an artistically arranged selection of tippets of black fur, black leather gloves, and lace-edged mourning handkerchiefs. As a *pièce de résistance* at the end of the counter farthest from the door lay black mourning arm bands and a scattering of black felt diamonds ready to be stitched onto the jackets and coats of a grieving public.

Feeling some obligation to comment on this impressive if slightly ghoulish and overdone presentation, Meg blurted out: "My word, Miss Martin … er … I should say, Petronella, you have been busy. Never in my life have I seen … such a … well! I suppose the word I am seeking is such an *outstanding* display. I'm sure our customers too will be very impressed."

Miss Martin gave a wintry smile and a regal nod of her head. "Thank you, Meg, although I am bound to say I did not create this artistic setting with the sole intention of impressing anyone. No. No! I feel it is the least I can do to show respect for our wonderful, compassionate, dear-departed Queen."

While privately wondering what precisely the Good Queen, who was reputed to have hated her Second City of the Empire, had ever done for the starving multitudes in the rat-ridden Glasgow hovels, Meg thought it best to keep her own counsel. She merely nodded somewhat absently as she set to work.

*Well*, Meg thought, *staunch dyed-in-the-wool disloyal, anti-monarchist or not, the way I'm feeling right now with my own raft of problems, at least my face will give the impression of deepest misery. If any one of our customers – or Petronella herself – chooses to equate my mournful expression with deep sadness at the passing of our late, lamented, revered, and over-indulged Britannic Majesty then jolly good luck to them.*

# Chapter 9

***Spring 1902***

Meg hummed quietly to herself as she went about her usual chores in preparing the shop for the business of the day ahead.

An involuntary smile rose to her lips as she thought: *For once life seems to be much better. Not only is old Mrs Martin in a better frame of mind and slightly more amenable to my helpful suggestions these days, but also the new arrangement allowing me to meet up with Nellie and Becky on Glasgow Green on my half days, weather permitting, seems to be working smoothly, so far at least.*

Petronella interrupted Meg's thoughts with: "Is it a private matter or may I join in, Meg?"

Meg roused herself sufficiently to reply: "Sorry. What was that? I didn't quite catch your meaning."

Petronella laughed. "I can't say I'm surprised. You were miles away, grinning all over your face. So, what's the joke? Surely it can't just be this lovely April day that has so lifted your spirits."

Meg laid down the duster she had in her hand on the counter. "Well, it goes without saying, Spring is my favourite season of the year, but yes, you're quite right, there is something else … a couple of things actually."

Petronella stood head cocked to one side as she waited to hear Meg's announcement, while Meg mentally debated just how much of her news she should reveal.

At last Meg gave a quick nervous cough. "First of all and uppermost in my mind is the fact that your mother and I do seem to be getting on a great deal better of late."

"Yes," Petronella nodded, "I have noticed a big improvement. Mother now seems more at ease with herself and not nearly so quick to take offence or fly into temper tantrums. I would be the first to admit that that's all thanks to you, Meg."

Meg demurred graciously at the compliment and Petronella went on: "But I interrupted you. You said there were two things."

Meg gave a mischievous grin. "If we're doing a stocktaking of the good things in my life right now, actually I should have said three not two."

"Now you've really got me intrigued. Do tell."

"If you're sure you can stand the excitement … This coming Saturday, Jack Dunn, you remember we mentioned him before? We've been meeting each other at almost all church social functions this last year and a bit – and not by accident! Well, he's invited me out for tea at Miss Cranston's. He's arranged to meet me in town after he's been to the football at Ibrox and later on we plan to go to a church soirée."

"At last! I knew things would brighten up when you started to take the advice I gave you long ago, even before you moved in with us. Splendid! Just one thing – I hope you won't be rushing into a whirlwind marriage or any such elopement to Gretna Green too soon. Mother and I would miss you."

Meg gave a hearty laugh. "It's early days yet, Petronella, so no need to worry on that score. Now, I'd better get back to work. You're not paying me good money just to stand about here chatting."

Petronella put out a detaining hand. "Not so fast, young lady. I've still to hear about your third item of good news."

Meg frowned suddenly aware of how close she'd come to disclosing details of Wee Becky's domestic arrangement.

On the instant, she decided to fob off her employer with harmless trivia about the new dress she had bought for Saturday's big event. However, as she started speaking the ping of the shop bell disturbed them.

Petronella gave a rueful smile. “I’ll hear about your new outfit later, Meg. For now it’s back to work for both of us.”

# Chapter 10

Saturday came at last and in honour of the great occasion Petronella even allowed Meg an extra half-day off to get her hair done and perhaps have time for a spot of window shopping in town before meeting up with Jack.

As Meg walked the length of Sauchiehall Street, despite knowing it to be the height of vanity, she could not resist admiring her newly-coiffeured image in the many shop windows lining the world-famous thoroughfare. On all sides were fur-coated matrons, who, judging by their self-satisfied airs and the number of expensive carrier bags they carried, had obviously done rather more than the expense-free window shopping Meg had indulged in. As she looked with interest at the scene around her she was struck by the fact that although the centre was busy, women, fur-coated or otherwise, were certainly in the majority. Apart from the occasional, obviously henpecked husband being trailed along on his wife's manic shopping spree there was scarcely a man, eligible or otherwise, to be seen anywhere.

Enjoying to the full the luxury of the unexpected hours of freedom from work Meg decided to do the entire traditional Glasgow outing of 'Up Sauchie and doon Buchie'. As she left Sauchiehall Street and strolled down the equally prestigious Buchanan Street she played her own private, harmless game of looking for further examples of henpecked husbands to add to her growing list. Halfway down Buchanan Street, having had her fill of window shopping and wishing to rest her tired feet, she decided to treat herself to afternoon tea.

Seated in the cosy tearoom and having already decided how many of the mouth-watering delicacies she could afford from the three-tiered cake-stand, she remarked to the waitress: “Not too many men indulging in afternoon tea, are there? It rather looks as if we’ve got it all our own way today.”

The frilly lace cap quivered on top of the grey-haired bun as the waitress chortled: “Aye, yer deid right therr, hen. They’ll all be ower yonder at Ibrox, like a lot o daft wee boys, shoutin their lungs oot for tae cheer on the Scotland team, so they will.”

Meg nodded, light dawning at last. “Oh, of course. I knew there was a match on but I’d forgotten it was such a big match – Scotland versus England!”

“Weel, hen, if you’ve forgotten aboot it, ye must be the only one in the whole country. One wey and another, they reckon there’ll be mair than 70,000 fans at Ibrox this day. But listen, Ah’d better scoot aff and get yer wee pot o tea or ma boss’ll be checkin me again for talkin ower much tae customers. See her! She’s aye sayin: ‘Now then, Euphemia, less talk, more walk.’”

On the point of turning away, the waitress bent over and whispered in Meg’s ear: “Listen, hen, when ye’re pickin yer dainty bites frae the cake-stand, tak ma advice and steer clear o them pineapple tarts. Rotten, so they are. Been sittin there since last Monday. See me, Ah widnae put tooth intae them, so Ah widnae.”

With these words of warning, a wink, and a wicked gleam in her eye – her duty done to a fellow worker on life’s journey – the waitress scooted off.

# Chapter 11

Meg's head was still buzzing with scraps of overheard conversational titbits from her fellow diners in the tearoom as she had a final aimless wander through the overheated and heavily perfumed shops at the bottom of Buchanan Street. Then at last it was time. Time to go along to the pre-arranged spot in bustling Argyle Street where she was to meet up with Jack Dunn. Rounding the corner she was not surprised to find that Glasgow's favourite rendezvous was already crowded with young women. Situated near the famous Hielanman's Umbrella, the designated meeting place, like a magnet, drew to itself couples who were already walking out or were about to embark hopefully on the courting circuit as the first stage on the sea of matrimony. In the usual, long established, but universally misunderstood, Glasgow camaraderie of talking in confidence to complete strangers it was no surprise that within minutes Meg found herself deep in conversation with two of the other women.

After exchanging the usual pleasantries regarding the weather, one of Meg's new-found friends said: "Weel, here's hoping ma lumber turns up. Ah don't know him all that weel. Just met him last week at a church soirée that ma Ma dragged me along tae. She's that desperate tae find me a man and for tae get me aff her hauns."

General laughter greeted this comment then an auburn-haired girl gave a bitter laugh. "Aye, fine weel dae ah ken whit ye mean on both counts. No only is ma Mammy goin aff her heid in case

Ah end up an auld spinster o the parish, but Ah got a real dizzy last Saturday nicht when ma lumber didnae gee hissell aboot turning up tae meet me."

Another girl joined in. "Uch, listen, hen, if ye got a dizzy yer no the first and Ah'm damn sure ye'll no be the last. So jist join the rest o the human race and stop girnin aboot it. It happened again tae me a couple o weeks back. No only did the eejit no come that nicht but Ah havenae even saw the bastard since."

Meg despite her prissy upbringing knew enough of the Glasgow parlance to realise a "lumber" was a boyfriend and that a "dizzy" referred to the acute disappointment when a promised date did not put in an appearance. This was the ultimate social shame for any self-respecting young Glasgow woman. For several minutes the trio discussed this topic before launching into a subject dearer to their hearts – the latest fashions.

The auburn-haired girl peeled herself off the shop window she'd been leaning against. She smoothed down her skirt, titivated her hair and with a look of triumph at her companions laughed. "Looks like Ah'm in luck the nicht. Here comes ma lumber aw decked oot like a fish supper. Cheerio then girls – Ah hope youse'll be lucky tae."

Linking arms with her swain as if to establish her territorial rights and thus warn off any predatory females they walked off already deep in conversation. Unexpectedly they stopped. The young man pointed back towards the other girls and as if having reached a decision he took a step in their direction as though intending to speak to them. His girlfriend physically held him back shaking her head.

Meg couldn't be altogether sure but she thought she heard the girl say: "Uch, jist leave them, Donald. If that's the lie o the land, poor souls, they'll find oot soon enough."

Still waiting patiently for Jack, Meg wondered at the strange behaviour of the couples as men arrived, obviously from the football match, to meet their girls. The pleased greeting from the girls wasn't matched by a similar salutation from the boyfriends.

Instead each couple was quickly involved in a conversation which, if facial expressions were anything to go by, was of a serious nature. Meg couldn't hear any of the words spoken clearly and dismissed the puzzle from her mind to concentrate on her own problem – where on earth was Jack?

A shiver of dismay went through her. *Surely she wasn't about to be the only girl left unattended on this street corner visibly announcing to the world she was the latest recipient of the dreaded 'Glesga Saturday nicht Dizzy'.*

A touch on her arm startled her.

"Listen, hen, don't think we're interferin or nothin, but are ye still waiting for yer man?" It was the young man of a couple who had spoken.

Meg, ever sensitive to her status as a *fallen woman,* thinking she was about to be warned of the dangers to a single woman standing alone on a street corner, bridled.

"What business is it of yours?"

"Therr's mibbe somethin ye should know." The young man said. "Wis yer fella goin tae the big match afore meeting ye?"

"Yes, as a matter of fact he was. He was going to Ibrox with his cousin. Why, do you know them?"

The young couple exchanged a meaningful look and the young lad went on: "Naw … the thing is …"

"Oh for God's sake spit it oot. Tell her." The girl snapped.

"There's been an accident, a terrible accident. Ah wis at Ibrox … a bit o the terracing gave way … lots o folk hurt. Doctors, ambulance men, Polis aw ower the place … Ah even saw one poor soul, lying on the ground breathing his last …"

The girl gripped Meg's arm.

"He disnae mean tae upset ye, hen. After aw it's took this yin aw this time tae get here whit wey there being crowds of folk aw trying tae get away and ambulances jamming up the place …"

"Right," the lad said. "Ah'm no for a minute saying yer fella's amang the injured … or even …"

His girlfriend jabbed her elbow into his ribs.

"If ye've waited this long, hen, and he hasnae turned up, mibbe ye'd best jist get alang hame. Chances are he'll turn up there right as rain."

With a heavy heart Meg walked unsteadily away.

# Chapter 12

Meg spent a sleepless night tossing and turning on her tear-damp pillow as she fretted about Jack and worried endlessly over what might have happened to him. What made matters worse was she had no means of getting in touch with him. She didn't even, after all the time she'd known him, have the slightest idea of where he and his mother lived.

In a limbo of numbing doubt and anxiety she finally fell into a troubled sleep on the thought: *Surely tomorrow at church I'll get some news – be it good or bad.*

Sunday dawned bright and sunny. It seemed to Meg, given the city-wide misery of the appalling disaster at Ibrox on Saturday, this brilliant April day was an obscenity and this burst of early spring sunshine did nothing to raise her spirits. Unable to lie in bed any longer she rose much earlier than was usually necessary, dressed quickly, and arrived outside the church well ahead of the time for the service. However, she was not alone in being ridiculously early. Obviously she was not the only person in the City of Glasgow who had spent a sleepless night and was now seeking comfort in the familiar ritual of the eleven o'clock service.

Meg settled herself in her usual pew and nodding, "good morning" to her neighbours, thought: *Anyone seeing me behaving normally like this would think I hadn't the slightest care in the world. If only they knew the turmoil I'm going through.*

However, well trained in the niceties of church behaviour Meg knew better than to crane her neck round to see other parishioners as they entered, so she was glad her habitual pew was close to the back row of the church.

*At least I'll be able to see almost everyone as they come in,* she thought. But she knew in her heart it wasn't *everyone* she was concerned about.

One by one the congregation filed in and there was still no sign of Jack or his mother. Meg could feel her spirits sinking under a rising tide of despair. At last, when she had all but given up hope, she saw Mrs Dunn being ushered in by her ever attentive son.

For once ignoring the protocol of proper church behaviour Jack, on spotting Meg, smiled and as he passed her sitting at the end of her pew slipped a folded piece of paper into the palm of her hand.

A quick glance round at her nearest neighbours reassured Meg that no-one had appeared to notice Jack's sleight-of-hand, but she was left with the dilemma of how to read the note without attracting attention to herself. After offering up a prayer of thanks for Jack's obvious safe deliverance from the football match disaster, Meg asked the forgiveness of the Almighty for what she was about to do. The very moment that the first hymn was announced, under cover of the rustle of the pages of many hymn books being turned, Meg unfolded and smoothed out the secret note and placed it unobtrusively on top of the designated hymn.

As Meg's lips moved only she, and the Almighty, knew it was not the words of the hymn she was mouthing as she avidly read the words on Jack's note.

# Chapter 13

At tea-break on the Monday morning Petronella and Meg discussed yet again at length the events of the weekend as they had affected the Glasgow public. So far Meg had managed to keep private her own immediate concerns.

"Didn't you say your young man had been planning to go to that match at Ibrox before meeting you?" Petronella said. "I'm sure that was what you told me, but with Mother listening I rather got the impression you did not want to upset her unnecessarily with your own involvements in the tragedy."

"Yes, but thanks be to God, he was one of the lucky ones. He wasn't hurt or injured in any way. Although it did rather change our plans for the evening."

"I would think it would. No doubt he was very shaken. I mean to say, witnessing a tragic event like that would not exactly be anyone's best moment. An evening of high tea and dancing would then be the last thing on his mind."

"No, you don't understand. What cancelled our plans was quite different. I didn't even get to meet Jack on Saturday. He stayed behind at Ibrox to help the injured while they were waiting for attention from doctors and ambulance men."

"Well, all I can say is this … that Jack of yours must be a very caring and compassionate young man putting aside his own safety, convenience, and social plans like that for the good of others."

"He's not exactly *my* Jack –"

"Listen to me Meg and listen well. Good men are hard to find, so just you see and hang onto him. Don't let *him* go pioneering off all footloose and fancy-free to the colonies."

Meg could feel the colour drain from her face and her hands shook.

*Had she imagined the subtle emphasis on the* him *in that last sentence? Does Petronella know my guilty secret? Has she found out the truth about the wastrel who fathered my wee Becky before beating a retreat to some far flung outpost of the Empire?*

"Er … um … Petronella, how do you mean pioneering off to the colonies?"

Petronella gave an impatient toss of her head. "Honestly, Meg. No need to look so worried. I'm not for an instant suggesting that *this young man* has already booked his passage on the next available emigrant ship. Really, you are the limit."

*Surely if she knew, Petronella would have me out of her house, and her employ, in short order. I must be imagining the emphasis. It's all in my guilty mind.*

"I'm still not quite sure what you're on about …"

Petronella gave a somewhat patronising smile. "Meg, really. Don't you ever read the morning newspapers? Almost every day the papers are full of those enticing advertisements offering anything up to a hundred and sixty acres of land absolutely free to anyone willing and able to sail off from Scotland and start a new life in Canada."

"Oh, yes. I do know what you mean now. I have seen those adverts and not only for Canada; Australia gets a mention too, I believe."

"That's right. And it isn't only skilled men they want. Anyone willing to work as farmhands, and healthy women are needed to work as domestic servants."

Meg sighed in relief. *Obviously, Petronella was talking in general terms. The emphasis had been in my mind and Petronella knew nothing about Becky and my past. The sooner I'm a decently married woman the better, and I won't have to go through the agonies of worrying about someone chancing on my secret.*

# Chapter 14

The chaste courtship of Meg and Jack was not without its upsets.

The week after the aborted tea at Miss Cranston's, Meg had her first invitation to visit Jack's home and meet his widowed mother. Mrs Dunn turned out to be a spoiled, selfish old woman whose behaviour and attitude towards Meg made it very clear that come hell or high water, she, as matriarch of the family, was determined to hang on to her beloved son. Subsequent visits did not improve the relationship as Mrs Dunn gave the impression that although Meg was well-spoken and well-mannered, a shop-girl was not a suitable match for her bank-clerk son.

Meg pressed her lips together and her knuckles showed white as she recalled in detail the events the spiteful old woman had, in one snide way or another, managed to ruin for them since their first introduction five months before. But yet again Meg had high hopes that tonight would be different …

Both Meg and Jack had been looking forward to the choral concert in the City Hall for which Jack had managed to get two of the very scarce tickets. At the prospect of an entire evening with Jack all to herself and thus well clear of his mother's apron strings Meg hummed happily. Jack had also suggested it would be pleasant to start off their evening by having high tea in the prestigious Ca'dora restaurant.

Although Jack in his usual quiet, unassuming way had made no other comment about his plans for the evening. Meg could not help feeling that perhaps this would be the night…

*Surely a proposal of marriage would at last be forthcoming?* Meg frowned as she thought of the other false alarms of the last few months, but tonight was her birthday, surely a good omen.

Meg grinned at herself in the mirror as she gave a final pat to her hair.

*Yes, my girl ... tonight's the night.*

Jack was already seated at a table and rose as Meg entered the room, waving her across. The first thing Meg noticed was that the table had three place settings, not two.

*Oh, well,* she thought, *Jack probably didn't have the foresight to ask for a romantic twosome and this was the table he was shown to.*

She settled herself comfortably and was just about to put her handbag on the empty chair when she heard Jack say: "Aha! Here she comes. The lady herself."

Meg turned to look at who was coming and Jack went on: "Are you all right, mother? You seemed rather a long time in the lady's powder room."

With a victorious smile at Meg, Mrs Dunn reached forward and, as if he were a naughty schoolboy, ruffled his hair with the words: "Silly boy. Always worrying about your poor old mum. I don't know *what* I'll do with you, Jackie."

She turned to Meg and twittered on: "He does worry so … all this fuss. Just a little headache, nothing to speak of."

Meg on the point of blurting out: "Then why bother to mention it, if it's that unimportant?" was saved the disgrace as Mrs Dunn continued: "No, I told Jackie a little thing like a headache wasn't going to stop me from joining you both for tea … especially when it's such a *special* evening … your birthday tea!"

The last comment was delivered with such a ring of triumph that Meg felt she was about to be physically sick. The idea of sharing the meal with the possessive old harridan was more than she could bear.

Meg slowly rose to her feet and looking down on mother and

son more in sorrow than in anger said: "You know what, Mrs Dunn, I do believe there's an epidemic of sick headaches going the rounds at the moment and it now seems to be my turn."

She turned to Jack. "Sorry about this, Jack. I'm sure your mother, herself a martyr to headaches, will fully understand my situation. Anyway you only have two tickets for the concert. So please, you and your mother enjoy both the concert and the meal. Goodnight."

With her head held high and, she hoped, her dignity intact Meg made her way out of the restaurant. Walking along the bustling city-centre street Meg was aware that in delivering both an unspoken ultimatum and a challenge, she had taken the risk of terminating the ongoing courtship and putting an end to the possibility of eventual marriage to her dear Jack.

# Chapter 15

To Meg's embarrassment and Petronella Martin's delight, the very next evening after the disastrous tea at the Ca'dora, Jack arrived on the Martin doorstep with a request to see Meg in private. Petronella ushered him into the parlour and rushed to Meg's room with the news.

Jack apologised profusely about the fiasco. It had not been his intention to have his mother there for the tea, but she had invited herself and he hadn't known how to say no. It wouldn't ever happen again.

To Meg's utter astonishment. Petronella bustled in with a silver tea-tray set for two and, having placed it before them, with a conspiratorial smile at Meg left them alone.

Meg started to pour tea then almost dropped the pot as Jack sank to his knees.

"Meg, my dear, will you do me the honour of being my wife?"

Meg quickly put down the pot. "Oh, Jack, do get up! Yes, I'll marry you."

Petronella, who must have had her ear pressed to the door, erupted in. "Meg! Congratulations. This calls for something a little more than tea, I think. Would you get the good sherry glasses from the dining room, Meg, and I'll fetch the decanter."

At her next visit to Nellie, Meg eventually scraped up enough courage to ask the question that had been troubling her.

Nellie listened to Meg's hesitant and circuitous preamble for a time then said: "Are ye tryin tae tell me yer thinkin o gettin married? That wid certainly be news tae me."

"No … it's just that … well … there is a chap who seems to be rather keen on me and … well … yes … he has asked me … but the thing is … if I did get married, would my husband know on the wedding night … I mean …"

Nellie roared with laughter. "Aw right, ye neednae spell it oot for me. Onywey, who's the lucky man?"

Meg, relieved that Nellie obviously did not require any further intimate details, rushed on: "He sits near me in church – it's Jack Dunn –"

Nellie's eyes opened wide in amazement. "Ye mean the son o auld Dragon Dunn? Oh, my God, he must be feeling his oats if he's darin tae look at ony woman, especially if his auld witch o a mither's in tow."

Meg had no answer to this and waited for Nellie to go on.

"Mind you, Meg, come tae think on it, leavin his mither aside, Jack Dunn would suit ye fine … him no bein experienced wi wimen like."

Meg held out a restraining hand.

Nellie grinned. "Listen, hen, Jack Dunn would be ideal husband material for ye. So jist ye gae ahead. A real do-gooder Ah hear, so come the weddin night if he *did* think awthin amiss … ye could aye say ye'd done ower much bicyclin."

Nellie gave a coarse laugh. "At the end o the day it's jist ye and me that kens the word for whit ye done – and it's naethin tae dae wi time spent cyclin."

# Chapter 16

***February 1903***

Now that Meg was married to Jack there wasn't a day that she didn't count her blessings. Her days of going to work in the haberdashery were finally behind her. At first she had worried about being able to pay Nellie, but Jack had been used to turning over his pay packet to his mother and handed it to Meg to deal with the household accounts. The weekly amounts to Nellie Meg could afford by being careful with her housekeeping and Jack was none the wiser. Even though she enjoyed being a housewife, Meg had to admit to herself, when the hated chore of ironing awaited her attention she was the first to invent an excuse to skive off and get as far away as possible from the mountain of crumpled clothes.

She hummed quietly to herself as she dusted round the living room, impatiently stowed away a bundle of darning, and plotted her escape for the rest of the day. After toying with, then dismissing, the idea of paying another visit to Nellie and Becky she finally settled on a visit to her church friend Anna Weir.

*Yes, the very idea. It's been a while since I visited Anna. I'll pop over there this afternoon.*

As she set out on her way through the city streets the sky was overcast and the first spots of rain were already gaining strength. By the time she reached Anna's home in Rutherglen Meg was soaked. Anna took one look at Meg when she answered the bell and burst out laughing.

"Meg, it's yourself. Well, dear, I would say that you're a sight for sore eyes – but the truth is you look like nothing other than a drowned rat. Come away in, into the warm."

They giggled like a pair of schoolgirls. Seated by the kitchen fire Meg said: "You know, I've always said that January was my most hated month, but this February with this downpour ... words fail me."

"You know you're more than welcome, of course, any time, but what on earth possessed you to come out on such a day?"

Meg gave a sheepish grin. "Apart from avoiding some household chores, I wanted to see you and in any case the weather wasn't too bad when I set out."

As if on cue there was a blattering of rain against the window.

Anna grinned. "At least you're home and dry for the moment. Now then, what's new since I last saw you?"

Meg shrugged. "Nothing much but ..." She nodded at the very obvious bulge under Anna's pinny. "... it looks to me as if you've got something exciting that I haven't heard about yet."

The rest of the afternoon was spent in pleasant chit-chat and fond reminiscences of their tried and tested friendship dating from the days when in trying to establish her image of respectability Meg had joined Anna in the church flower rota.

Battling her way against the driving rain and splashing through the puddles on her way home Meg felt an inner glow of happiness.

*I'm so pleased for Anna, she's going to be a mother at last. Poor soul, I think she'd almost given up all hope of ever achieving that dream.*

Next day when Jack arrived home for his mid-day meal he flourished his morning paper. "Looks like you were lucky to get safely home yesterday from your visit to Rutherglen. The paper's full of it. Seems yesterday's rainstorms were the worst in living memory. The whole of Scotland was affected ... flooding everywhere, livestock swept away ... as for Glasgow itself–"

Jack paused for breath and Meg said: "I know I got well and truly soaked, but apart from that–"

Jack smiled as his meal was placed before him. "Here, dear, read all about it for yourself – seems that every river in Glasgow bust its banks: the Clyde, the Cart, and the Kelvin. You were lucky to get home safely without too much upset. Never mind, you had a good heart-to-heart blether with Anna. I know you've missed her since she moved to that church nearer her new home."

# Chapter 17

***October 1903***

Approaching their first anniversary, Meg and Jack appeared to all as a settled, albeit rather staid, couple. As yet there were still no signs of any addition to their family except for a very bad-tempered canary rejoicing in the name Pretty Boy. The bird was as spoiled as any doted-upon, longed-for child and ruled the roost in the Dunn household. Not only did he have his likes and dislikes but he had a positive aversion to the sound of anything sizzling in the frying pan. Meg was cooking Jack's ritual Sunday morning fry-up and Pretty Boy was hopping to and fro in his version of a childish tantrum when Jack entered the kitchen.

"Still up to his tricks, I see," Jack said and planted a chaste kiss on Meg's cheek.

"If anyone had told me there was such a thing as a bad-tempered canary I'd have told them to pull the other leg."

Jack laughed. "You're right, dear. If ever we should hear the patter of tiny feet, Pretty Boy's beak would surely be out of joint. Mad with jealousy he'd be."

After church, when the minister had given the pulpit rail its weekly hammering, on their way home Jack said: "Meg, are you quite sure you don't want to come with me this afternoon?"

"I'll leave it for this week, if you don't mind, dear. After all, it isn't even as if you mother knows who I am. You've said it yourself – there are times when she scarcely recognises even you."

"That's true enough I suppose. You know, no matter how I wrack my brains, I'll just never understand what brought on mother's stroke. I always took such good care of her. Not a worry in the world, did she have, not a single worry."

Meg made no reply. Although there was plenty she could have said to throw light on the matter, her lips were sealed.

When the silence was growing uncomfortable Meg squeezed Jack's arm and said: "No, best that you go on your own today. I'll give you some of those wee sponge fingers to take along. Even on her bad days she always likes them. Soft on the gums, aren't they?"

Having seen Jack safely off on his duty visit Meg was settling down at the fireside with a welcome cup of tea when the doorbell interrupted her solitude. When she opened the door to admit Nellie, she pushed her way past Meg in the narrow hallway and marched straight into the kitchen.

"What brings you out on such a day, Nellie? Look at you; you're drenched to the skin. Here, give me your shawl. I'll hang it up on the pulley."

Divested of her shawl and seated at the fire with a cup of tea and a buttered pancake on a plate beside her, Nellie seemed a little more at ease. Even so, she looked round then in a stage whisper asked: "Is his lordship ben the room wi his books?"

Meg shook her head. "No, he's gone to visit his mother."

Nellie snorted in disgust. "Oh, her! Don't tell me she's still hingin on in that church home for the aged and infirm. She's the very one that'll cling tae life tae the bitter end – especially if, in the process, she can make everyone else's life a misery, if no an actual livin hell."

Meg gave a wintry smile. "Oh, I think you're perhaps exaggerating a little, Nellie. The poor old woman. She can't help being ill and landing up in that home."

"Puir auld woman, ma fit! And don't ye gae changin yer tune. Who was it telt me it wis the shock o her darlin son haein the temerity tae git merit that gave her the stroke in the first place? The very thought o her wee boy lyin wi a woman damned near killed her."

Meg felt herself pale. “Nellie! I told you that in confidence.”

“Aye, aye, keep yer shirt on. Ah didnae come here the day tae talk aboot auld Dragon Dunn. Ah’ve got mair important things on ma mind than yon selfish auld bitch.”

Meg bridled. “I’ll thank you not to use such language in my house, Nellie. It’s well seen that you don’t go to church.”

Nellie banged down her plate on the wee creepie stool with such force that the half-eaten pancake almost fell off onto the rag rug before the hearth.

She glared at Meg. “That’s right, hae a go at me noo because Ah don’t sit every Sunday under the Reverend C Semple Armstrong. Weel, if the truth be telt, Ah’m far tae busy bringin up ma squad o weans, no tae mention wipin the bum and moppin up the sick o yer ain wee bastard – far tae busy daein aw that for tae waste time listenin tae yon high-falutin meenister dronin on week efter week.”

Having delivered herself of this diatribe Nellie sat back and again glared at her sister as if now issuing an unspoken but very real challenge.

Meg, still mentally reeling from her sister’s outburst, felt a reply of some sort was now expected of her. She cleared her throat twice before saying: “I must say you’re in a very strange mood today, Nellie. Even so, I can’t believe you braved the downpour to trail round here to the Parliamentary Road with the sole purpose of shouting such abuse at me.”

Nellie banged her clenched fist on the arm of the chair. “Damned right! Aye there was somethin Ah had tae tell ye, but we’ll let that flea stick tae the wall for noo. Ah’ll come tae that later. In the meantime, ye can collect yer bastard ony time ye like and bring her here to live with yer beloved Jack.”

Meg was stunned with this bolt from the blue, but Nellie went on: “Aye, that’s the ploy. Ye can explain it onywey ye like tae yer darlin man.”

By now, with her mind and emotions in a turmoil, Meg could feel the fabric of her settled married life collapse around her. No matter how she pleaded with Nellie her sister was adamant. Even the offer of an extra half-crown a week didn't sway her; she'd had more than enough of looking after Becky.

"But why? Why now, Nellie? What on earth am I to tell Jack? How can I possibly explain away Becky?"

"Ye can tell him ony damn thing ye like, hen. Ah don't mind if ye tell him the truth aboot how ma ain situation has changed – it'll be plain tae see soon enough."

"Changed? In what way are things now so different? Just tell me that."

"Oh, Ah'll tell ye aw right. Noo that Rab's hame mair often he's at it every five minutes, isn't he? Ah've fallen again, haven't Ah? Wi naethin happenin the last couple o years Ah thocht Ah wis past it. But naw, trust ma luck, Ah'm the one tae be haein a change-o-life baby!"

"A baby! At your age?"

"Meg, wid ye please stoap repeatin everythin efter me. Ye're beginnin tae sound like that daft budgie ye both dote on. Aye, Ah'm carryin in ma belly a change-o-life baby and wance it's born Ah'll hae enough on ma plate without fleein daft efter a toddler as weel."

In the silence that followed Nellie rose to her feet. "Noo, if ye'll jist get ma shawl doon aff yer pulley Ah'll be on ma wey. Rab's hame for a couple o days and daein his nut aboot another baby. Between him and the weans runnin wild the place will be in an uproar."

Meg handed Nellie the still damp shawl and Nellie said in a more kindly tone: "Mibbe things'll workout for the best. Onywey, when Ah've gone just sit yersell doon and get clear in yer mind whit ye'll be tellin Jack. Weel, cheerio, hen. Sorry if Ah've disturbed the peace of yer Sunday efternoon."

# Chapter 18

For the remainder of that memorable afternoon Meg agonised over her quandary. There was simply no way she could announce the facts to her husband. If she did, her comfortable marriage to the steady, reliable, if somewhat boring, Jack would be well and truly consigned to the scrapheap of life.

*What in God's name was she expected to do or say?*

Determined to keep focussed and busy, Meg bustled round the house dusting this, re-arranging that, and generally creating work and chaos where previously none had existed.

So it was when Jack came home he returned to a scene of domestic bliss where, for some strange reason, not only had the furniture been re-positioned, but every item from brass candlesticks to decorative soup tureens, to china ornaments had been cleaned and polished for dear life. A roaring fire whose flames licked up the chimney warmed the room and his wife, pristine as the china crinoline ladies in the display cabinet sat meekly by the fireside diligently working on a piece of crochet.

Meg raised her head and smiled. "Your tea's nearly ready, dear. It's your favourite – toad-in-the-hole. But first, how was your mother? Any improvement in her condition?"

Jack sighed. "Improvement did you say? Hmph! If anything she was even worse today. She moaned about everything, nothing pleased her, decided she hated sponge fingers. And just would not listen to reason on any subject. But worst of all–" Jack paused as if to gather the moral strength to continue with his tale of woe.

"You'll never believe it, Meg, but worst of all it was really bizarre, she actually thought I was her long dead brother, Ross! That's right, the black sheep of the family, a man whose guts she hated. A gambler, a womaniser and by all accounts no better than he should be. A man she couldn't stand and could never get along with."

Meg gave a sympathetic shake of her head.

"Yes," Jack went on, "I can honestly say that this afternoon's fiasco was without doubt the worst visit I've ever had with my mother. I tell you, Meg, and I wouldn't dream of breathing a word of this to another living soul … but the moment the bell went for the end of visiting time, it came as a blessed relief. That's the God's honest truth. I felt like an escaping prisoner."

Meg chewed at her lip, fully aware that now was definitely not the moment to spring on Jack her own dramatic news.

Later, with the tea things cleared away, and Meg and Jack sitting companionably on either side of the fire, Meg tentatively started to broach the subject which was uppermost in her mind. Feeling as if she was walking on eggs, Meg tiptoed her way round until she could no longer avoid the dénouement. Even then she knew she had to put forward her startling proposal in such a way as to make Jack think that any suggestion as to a possible solution to the problem had come from him.

Having laid some of the groundwork and given him time to mull it over she heard Jack say: "So, one way and another it hasn't exactly been the best of afternoons for either of us, has it, dear?"

With what she hoped was a brave smile Meg said: "Well, I have to admit, hearing all of my sister's worries certainly didn't make for cheery listening."

"Poor Nellie, she's really going to have her hands full isn't she? With her squad of children, Rab under her feet more often than not, and toddler Becky running around and into everything the last thing she needs is another baby. From what you say Nellie is feeling out of sorts and bitterly resenting her fate of becoming an old mother. Not a happy prospect, is it, my dear?"

Meg nodded. "If only there was some way we could help her,

Jack, lighten her burden, at least in some small measure. After all as good churchgoers we are only too aware that the minister is forever telling us to help our neighbours. Surely when it comes to family it is even more our Christian duty, don't you agree?"

Jack frowned in concentration then rose to the bait. His words came out in a rush. "My sentiments exactly, Meg. Now I don't know how you, or Nellie either for that matter, would take to this … but it seems to me that the older children won't pose as much of a problem as an active toddler who needs eyes in the back of the head attention, right?"

Meg nodded, already daring to hope for the impossible as the she waited for her husband to go on.

"Meg, you may not be aware of it, but I've seen the doting way you look at that lovely wee Becky any time she's been with us. A real wee charmer she is, and since as yet we've no children of our own and no sign of any immediate happy event how would it be if…"

Meg sagged with relief as she listened to Jack's master plan. Yet again her secret was safe.

*Panic over. Thank God. Nellie is sure to jump at Jack's kind offer and keep her own counsel as to Becky's true parentage. Thank you, thank you, God. It's a dream come true. I can have my own darling wee Becky at home to bring up properly.*

# Chapter 19

Even in the short time Becky had been with them, life had taken on a rosy hue of happiness in the Dunn household. Becky, doted on by her Uncle Jack and her Aunt Meg, was the centre of their universe. She was now approaching a milestone in her young life – her first day at the local primary school.

In preparation for starting school, Meg had taken Becky to the old teacher she had lived with when her parents died and who had ensured that Meg had grown up speaking 'properly'.

Miss Euphemia Edgar looked Becky over. "So this is the young lady for whom you gave up a promising career in teaching?"

For a moment Meg thought she had made a mistake in bringing Becky to meet Miss Edgar and that she had guessed Meg's secret.

However, Miss Edgar went on: "It was very noble and unselfish of you to give up your training to help your sister when she needed you. And now once again you are coming to her aid by taking care of her daughter. I suppose it was all for the best. You've married well to a young man with a promising future in the bank, and you certainly couldn't have continued teaching once you'd married."

She turned to Becky. "Now, young lady, your Aunt Meg tells me you are about to start school. You and I have some work to do on your speech before that great day."

Meg hoped that with this start and the example of Jack and herself, Becky would lose the coarse accent she had naturally acquired living with Nellie. Perhaps, Meg hoped, Becky would thus escape the fate of many pupils of being punished with the dreaded Lochgelly for not knowing they were expected to be bilingual and not to resort to the common language of the streets and their homes despite many of the words being perfectly respectable old Scottish words.

As far as Meg and Jack were concerned, as long as it was in their power to do so, Becky Bryden would have the best of everything life had to offer.

# Chapter 20

*Becky, fast approaching her seventh birthday, seemed to be growing in grace and beauty with each passing day …* so ran Meg's thoughts as she brushed out Becky's long ringlets. *And now thanks to Miss Edgar's friend Abigail Andrews, my old elocution teacher, Becky speaks clearly and well.* Meg felt a glow of pride at the way Becky Bryden was turning out.

*Yes,* thought Meg, *everything has ended up much better than either Nellie or I could ever have envisaged.*

Meg gave an involuntary shiver as she recalled that terrible morning of Becky's birth … the pain, the secrecy, the utter sordidness of it all even without the subterfuge and lies of the nine weary, long months preceding the birth itself.

Now she had a contented family life, mistress of her own home, with a husband who not only loved her but was also devoted to Becky. In the eyes of the world and their church-going friends they were doing their Samaritan best in helping out a poor overburdened relative.

Still in a rosy glow of happiness Meg allowed her thoughts to drift, to envisage an even brighter future in which Becky would fulfil Meg's lost dreams of becoming a teacher. A fully qualified, successful teacher …

# Part 2

## Chapter 1

*1 January 1914*

The day started as no other Becky Bryden had ever before experienced in her short life. When she opened her eyes at six o'clock, instead of the ritual cup of tea that her Aunt Meg had always handed in to her in the wall bed in their flat on the Parliamentary Road, she awoke to the feeling of a rough hand shaking her shoulder, the cold of a strange, unfamiliar room, and a voice shouting: "Right, Becky, get oota that scratcher. Therr's nae call for ye tae lie in yer bed all day. Ye're no an idle schoolgirl noo, and Ah'm no yer saft Aunt Meg."

If Becky had been trying to persuade herself that since she had left school the previous week her life had not changed dramatically, then this rude early morning awakening was enough, more than enough, to disillusion her. The dye was cast and despite how Aunt Meg and Becky's complacent, pipe-smoking Uncle Jack, and Becky herself had railed against it, Becky's mother had won the day.

The argument had been heated and decidedly acrimonious and Becky could still hear in her head her mother's strident voice.

"Rab said it was a mistake tae let Becky stay wi ye since she started school, but Ah wis sorry for ye. A puir barren childless woman and Ah had children tae spare even tho my last, wee Elspeth, died of the diphtheria when she wis four. But noo wi ma girls married and their pay packets gone, Rab no fit tae go tae sea and withoot a job, all Ah've left tae bring any money intae the hoose is Erchie. Ah need Becky tae come hame, get a job, and bring in some money. She *is* ma daughter efter all, isn't she?"

In this last sentence Becky had thought she had heard an unusual emphasis and couldn't understand why it had reduced Aunt Meg to tears and ended the argument. Of course Nellie Bryden was her mother. The school register recorded her parents as Mr and Mrs R Bryden, but her address had always been Aunt Meg's. No one to her knowledge had ever questioned the arrangement. Aunt Meg had been kind enough to take her in and feed and clothe her since she was four and Nellie, with her husband unemployed and a semi-invalid, had so many other mouths to feed.

Becky sighed and swung her legs out of bed into the cold room and whatever awaited her in the day ahead. Her mind still dwelt on the family row but more than anything it was the injustice of it all, the callous indifference to Becky's hopes and aspirations and the scant reward to Aunt Meg for her years of sacrifice and saving. The childless, caring woman had been more of a mother to her through her years of growing up than this harridan still bawling at her from the kitchen to: "… get a move on and get oot o that scratcher."

Chittering with cold as she flung on her clothes, Becky felt heat rise to her face in disgust as unbidden came the thought: *Can't she even use the proper word for bed?*

The use of the crude Glasgow vernacular together with the harsh guttural sounds of her mother's voice Becky felt were almost as much a physical blow to her as the sparse living conditions in which she now found herself. Since she had gone to live with Aunt Meg, Aunt Meg had insisted that she speak "proper English" and have no truck whatever with anything even remotely connected with "Glesga keelies."

*Yes,* Becky thought, *Aunty Meg had been grooming me to make something of my life. With a decent secondary school education and a fistful of higher leaving certificates under my belt, careful manners and the right 'bool-in-the-mooth' vowels, who knows where I might have ended? But not here! Most certainly not here!*

Becky was still attempting to button up her cardigan with fingers stiff with cold as she entered the only other room of the tenement flat. She raised her eyebrows in surprise at the welcome sight of a roaring fire in the grate, the table neatly set, and her mother in her long sackcloth apron stirring a bubbling porridge pot with a wooden spurtle.

"So! Ye're up at last are ye? Weel, sit yersel doon and get a guid gutful o porridge intae yer belly – for it's a gey cauld yin oot therr this mornin."

Becky squirmed inwardly then, feeling annoyed at herself for being so negative and judgemental, she tried to make amends.

"That's very kind of you, Mother. Yes, a bowl of porridge, that will do nicely. And how lovely it is to come into an already made and cheery welcoming fire."

Her mother raised her head and, giving Becky a baleful look, snapped: "Izzat ye trying for tae be cheeky, ma lass? And forbye therr's nae need for aw yer fancy manners in *this* hoose. Ye're no at yer Aunty Meg's noo."

The red-faced angry woman unceremoniously dumped a bowl of porridge on the table in front of Becky.

"Therr ye ur. But don't think Ah'll be makin yer porridge for ye every morn, nor even lightin the fire – that'll be yer job. While we're at it, ma fine Lady Becky, therr's nae need at aw for ye tae be cryin me 'Mothah', jist try sayin either Mammy or Mither, Ah'm no that fussed but for the love o the wee man, jist gie aw that la-di-dah stuff a rest."

Unsure how to respond to this tirade Becky simply nodded. This seemed to be all that was required of her. "Becky, lass, Ah'm only sayin these things for yer ain guid. Let's face it, hen, if ye dae manage tae get a job in the bakehoose, the rag store, or if ye're really lucky in Templeton's Carpet Factory, if ye keep on talkin all posh yer workmates wull make yer life a livin hell."

Becky placed her spoon on top of the porridge feeling that she had lost whatever slight appetite she had had. The mental image of the dismal future prospects being laid before her would have sickened a stronger constitution than hers.

"Thank you for your concern, Moth– er … Mammy. I'm sure you're right. In fact I know you are. Even at school the other pupils called me names."

Her mother gave as satisfied nod. "If ye kent the rows Ah've had wi that stuck-up Meg ower the way she was bringin ye up. Onywey, at least ye and me sees eye tae eye, so that's guid. Noo, sup up yer porridge and aff ye go. Ye're young, bright, and strong so therr's bound be some sort o job oot therr for ye. Jist jump at the furst job that offers ye the maist wages. People like us cannae afford tae pick and choose. Remember, if the Guid Lord had wanted for ye tae be a lady he widnae hae plunked ye doon here in a tenement flat in Brigton's Main Street."

# Chapter 2

As Becky left the small comfort and shelter of the common close on this cruelly cold January morning she shivered and pulled closer the ancient shawl her mother had insisted she wear.

Her mother had been adamant: "Aye, ye'll wear a shawl like aw the rest o us womenfolk hereaboots. Yer coat will be kept safe in mothballs and brocht oot o the wardrobe for the Kirk on the Sabbath. Onywey, face the facts, lassie, whit employer's gonnae offer ye a job if ye gae in lookin like some well-heeled toff frae the West End?"

As she pulled the moth-eaten garment closer and tighter round her neck, Becky had to admit that hating the shawl or not she was indeed glad of its all-embracing warmth. As she hurried along the London Road Becky knew that poorly clad as she was, not only did she blend well into the surging work force around her, she was only one of many such poverty-stricken Glasgow women destined to work all the hours a caring God sent in some lowly job and to count herself lucky to get a pittance for her labour.

With these gloomy thoughts Becky, head down against the biting wind, marched blindly along with the tide of humanity. A voice at her elbow caused her to raise her head at the same moment as a hand grasped at the fringes of her shawl.

"Ur ye daft or whit? Ye nearly got yer shawl ironed oot therr. No tae mention nearly meeting yer Maker."

Becky gave a puzzled frown and a workman leaning on his shovel said: "The lassie's right. She's jist saved yer life, so she did.

Ye near as dammit ended up under the hooves o that Clydesdale, no tae mention bein splattered oot under the coal cairt it's luggin roon the streets."

Becky found herself looking into the concerned eyes of the young woman who was still clutching the fringes of the hated shawl.

Before Becky could thank the woman for her help her saviour said: "Listen, hen, fine weel Ah ken it's wan hell o a mornin, but it's jist the same for the rest o us, so therr's surely nae call for ye tae go chuckin yersel under a coal-cairt. Ah mean tae say, things cannae be as bad as aw that, noo can they?"

Her rescuer had spoken in almost mocking tones and when Becky met her glance she felt herself match the spirit of merriment implied in the half-in-fun, whole-in-earnest delivery of the speech. As the relief at Becky's lucky escape and the utter stupidity of the situation dawned on them the girls smiled at each other.

"I do thank you," Becky said. "Had it not been for you and your gallant efforts – according to our friend the workman – I'd have been half way to the Royal Infirmary by now, if not heading for a slab in the morgue."

This praise served only to embarrass Becky's rescuer who gazed down at her booted feet and toed elaborate patterns in the tarmacadam of the pavement.

"Och, it wis nae bother, hen. Onytime."

At a loss to know what next to say to express her gratitude Becky said: "Anyway, thanks again. I just hope I haven't kept you late for your work."

The young woman raised her head. "Work, did ye say? Late for ma work? Chance would be a fine thing. If ye must ken, Ah'm job huntin. That's why ma mither has flung me oot o the hoose this early. She cannae thole for tae see me like aw ma brithers, idle, and no bringin intae the hoose as much as a fudgie for ma keep."

Becky at once felt a common bond with her rescuer especially as she knew the same could be said of herself – to date she had been unable to give her mother even the self-same fudgie, a miserly farthing, towards household expenses.

When Becky formally introduced herself to her new-found friend the girl said: “Och, jist caw me Caz. That’s aw Ah ever get. Ma mither must hae been aff her heid when she labelled me for life as Carolina Rose. She’s niver saw a rose in ony back court in Brigton and Ah dinnae think she’s ever been in spittin distance o anybody as exotic as Carolina.”

Becky hoped her smile was suitably sympathetic.

Caz exaggerated her very real shiver. “Ah don’t ken aboot ye, Becky, but Ah’m fair perished wi cauld.”

Becky nodded. “This windswept corner hasn’t got a lot going for it, has it? The problem now is; if we’re both looking for work, just where do we go from here?”

Caz frowned. “Weel, ye please yersel, china, but Ah kin tell ye wan thing – Ah’m no goin within a mile o the rag store. Ah kin get mair than enough fleas at hame withoot workin aw day wi the wee tormentors.”

“Can’t say I was too anxious to try for work there myself, nor even at Paddy’s Market. Also I’d rather give the bakehouse a miss as well. A neighbour warned me the night shift boss there is to be avoided at all costs as he is a lecherous old devil, or as she put it: A randy old bugger.”

“Ah couldnae hae put it better masel. It seems he’s that guid at the bakin, for want o another word for it, that he’s wantin tae put a bun in the oven o every daft new lassie that crosses his path and hisnae the guts tae tell the filthy auld groper tae take a runnin jump tae hissel.”

Although scandalised by the language she had just heard and the mental picture it had presented, Becky, while glad to have made a new friend, determined to stick to the subject of job hunting.

“Well then, Caz, apart from the coal yard or maybe even trundling round with a barrow helping the fishwife blow her bugle, I suppose that leaves us with only a couple of manufactories on the other side of Argyle Street – that or the carpet factory.”

Caz grinned. "Templeton's is nearer, so we'll try oor luck therr furst, eh, no?"

Assuming Becky was in complete agreement with this plan of action, Caz took hold of her arm and like a pair of old school chums they headed in the direction of Glasgow Green. Some fifteen minutes later as they approached the imposing, ornate building – Glasgow's look-alike Venetian palazzo – Becky felt her new-found confidence rapidly evaporate.

"Oh heavens! Would you look at it. Up close it looks really unapproachable – just like the king's palace. Sorry, Caz, I just wouldn't have the nerve to wander in unannounced and ask for work. I'd just shrivel up with embarrassment and be dumb with fright. I'd be a right bag of nerves."

"If ye think Ah saved yer bluidy life jist so ye could die o fright at the mercy o some mill gaffer, ye can think again."

With these words like a clarion call to arms, Caz all but frog-marched a trembling Becky into the overwhelming grandeur of Glasgow's palazzo whose outward appearance of ease, luxury, and indulgence belied the grim workplace within – Templeton's Carpet Factory.

# Chapter 3

Later that same evening in the tenement flat in Bridgeton's Main Street Becky was washing the dishes at the stone sink under the window while her mother sat crocheting by the fireside. Over in the set-in wall bed Becky's invalid father, snoring loudly, occasionally gave such an earth shaking snort that Becky was in danger of dropping the dish she was drying.

At just such a moment Erchie, Becky's elder brother, arrived home. As he entered the room in his coal-man's work garb of moleskin trousers, hessian apron with its leather overlay, and steel-tipped boots he staggered as he negotiated the short distance between the door and the other armchair.

Erchie collapsed in an untidy heap onto the chair, gave a gargantuan belch, slapped his stomach, and demanded: "Rich weel. So where's ma tea? Ah'm fair starvin, so Ah am. Ah could eat a scabby horse and come back for the driver."

Silence greeted this overworked Glasgow expression and when neither Becky nor his mother at once rose to do his bidding, he glowered first at one and then at the other female.

"Have youse gone deaf? Ah said, where's ma f***in tea? Ah've did a day's hard graft humpin bluidy bags o coal up hunners o stairs. Noo it's wimmen's work for tae bring me some belly timber."

When neither woman moved, he roared: "If ye don't ken a hungry man's an angry man, ye'll bluidy soon find oot. Forbye no one o ye has had the common decency for tae loosen aff ma boots for me."

Becky's heart sank as she looked at this stinking hulk of a man, a cruel bully, whose very presence seemed to fill the small room with an aura of menace. Unsure of her part in this domestic drama Becky waited with bated breath to see what her mother's actions or orders would finally be.

With great deliberation Mrs Bryden laid down her crochet on the creepie stool beside her chair, got slowly to her feet, then, standing before her son she peered down at him.

"If ye'd wanted yer tea, therr was a plate o pipin hot stovies on the table for ye at the appointed time – that was the time ye finished yer guid work. In case ye cannae count that was three bluidy hours ago."

Erchie opened his mouth to protest, but Mrs Bryden went on: "And while we're at it. If that's you back on the booze again then either you come for yer tea at the right time or ye can damn well whistle for it. Has that sunk into yer thick skull?"

A bleary-eyed Erchie gazed up at his mother, who gave him stare for stare in good measure. When it was clear he had lost this particular round of the domestic battle, like a petulant child determined to have his own way in at least one area of his life, Erchie said: "Aye, Ah hear ye, Mither. But that disnae answer ma ither question – whit aboot ma boots? They'll no take themselves aff ma f***in feet will they?"

Mrs Bryden pursed her lips, then called over to Becky: "Becky, fill the kettle and while it's comin tae the boil for a wee cup o tea for ye and me, Ye can tak aff Erchie's boots for him. Let the daft eejit sleep aff the booze in his chair."

As Becky bustled to do her mother's bidding it was with a heavy heart she realised that this disgusting chore would from now on be hers. Later, having filled a basin for Erchie to steep his foul-smelling feet, Becky, her mother, and a now sobering Erchie sat round the fire and sipped at their enamel mugs of strong tea. With a semblance of domestic peace at least temporarily restored Mrs Bryden turned to Becky.

"Weel noo, lassie. Ye micht as weel tell Erchie yer guid news. Its mair than high time we had a wee bit guid cheer in this hoose."

At these words Erchie raised his head.

"Are ye mibbe goin back tae the Parliamentary Road tae stay wi yer beloved Aunt Meg? Ah hope tae God, ye are. That wey Ah'll get ma ain bed back. For Ah don't mind tellin ye Ah'm gettin bluidy fed up sleepin – or at least tryin for tae sleep – on that decrepit wee creepie bed oot in the lobby."

Mrs Bryden frowned. "Ah'm gonnae nip that idea in the bud straight aff, Erchie. Ah'm tellin ye this; Becky's here tae stay. And before ye start arguin the toss wi me listen weel tae whit Ah'm tellin ye. Even though ye are brother and sister, it just wouldnae be seemly tae hae the pair o ye sharin the front room."

Erchie's eyes widened and he gave a snort of disgust.

"Seemly did ye say? Ye didnae worry aboot that, Mither, when therr was five o us sleepin head tae toe ben the room."

"Erchie, that's enough! Onywey, needs must when the devil drives and ye were aw younger then. But noo – weel the plain fact is ye're a man, six years older than Becky and with her noo mair like to a stranger than a sister …"

Mrs Bryden paused before she went on:

"In any case, Ah need Becky here tae help me in ma auld age. Ah'll need her pay packet as weel – especially if ye ever decide tae mak an honest woman o yer fancy piece in Landressy Street – her wi that brood o weans no single wan of which has the same faither. If ye gae aff tae the colonies wi her, ye'll need every bawbee ye can lay hands on. If Becky wisnae here therr widnae be a penny piece comin intae the hoose tae keep yer faither and me."

Becky had listened in horrified silence at the dirty linen being dragged out before her and at the prospect of her life to come. Mrs Bryden turned to her, a touch of asperity and rising impatience in her voice, and said: "Weel, Becky, ur ye gonnae tell Erchie yer guid news? Or dae we hae tae wait till the coos come hame afore ye put the puir fella oot of his misery?"

"It's like this, Erchie," Becky said. "My news is soon told. I've got a job and I start on Monday!"

# Chapter 4

In the closely-packed tenements of her native Glasgow, buildings alive with squads of children, the ongoing dramas of day-to-day living, the drunken brawling of frustrated, unemployed artisans, and the screams and arguments which ricocheted off the crumbling walls were a permanent feature of life. So common were these sounds, that the only time Becky noticed them was when, for some reason or other, there would be a lull in this vibrant heartbeat. At such times Becky would find herself almost holding her breath as she strained to hear the onset of the next bout of weeping, cursing or raucous singing of some staggering-home, drunken neighbour.

A somewhat lesser cacophony had been with her since early childhood and she had learnt to accept it as an essential element of tenement living. Strangely enough it was only after she had moved to stay with her mother in the Main Street flat that such noises had begun to annoy her in any way and then, as today, actually intrude on her sensibilities.

*This is ridiculous,* Becky thought for the tenth time in as many minutes, *the noises off are only different in scale and volume from those I regularly heard around at Aunt Meg's flat in the Parliamentary Road, so why am I making such a fuss now?*

Becky knew in her heart the answer to her question. She was desperately unhappy at having had, arbitrarily, to leave the comfort, the tender loving care of Aunt Meg's home. Not only was she depressed and miserable, but she knew she was hypercritical of everything in the Bryden's flat. To make matters worse she was keenly aware of how stressed and anxious she felt at the dawning of each new day in having to cope with her job at the carpet factory. If she were being honest with herself, Becky knew she was piling all her frustrations, uncertainties and misery onto the one element of her daily life at which she could openly rail and complain.

Sitting by the fireside trying to relax after yet another hard day's graft at Templeton's she heard the one sound which not only set her teeth on edge, but these days was slowly but surely driving her to very edge of insanity.

"Oh, no! Not again. Honestly, Mammy, I don't know how you can stand it. Can't you at least bang a broom handle on the ceiling? Let her know you are aware of the noise and that it is disturbing you?"

With a *tut* of annoyance Mrs Bryden laid down the sock she had been knitting.

"Becky, ye're the one with the ladylike feelins. So if the squeaky pulley from upstairs bothers ye that much, jist ye bang awa at the ceilin tae ye hert's content. But Ah'll tell ye this noo – it'll no dae ye, nor onybody else for that matter, one damned bit o guid. The auld besom will jist bang back doon tae us the then we'll hae e'en mair noise."

Becky sighed. "Well, then if that's the case, why on earth don't you tell her to her face? At least give her the chance to oil her pulley. Surely that's not too much to ask, now is it? Aunty Meg would never have put up with this. She would have resolved such a situation amicably at the very outset."

On the point of resuming her knitting, Mrs Bryden cast a baleful look over the top of her spectacles at the red-faced, irate Becky. "Oh, aye. Yer wonderful Aunty Meg, she could dae naethin wrang – no accordin tae ye anyroads. Weel, put it this wey, Ah'm no yer sainted Aunty Meg, but Ah'm enough o a guid neebor for tae realise it's no up tae me tae dictate tae ony auld widow woman, far less the Widow Wilson upsterrs, hoo tae spend her precious bawbees. Believe me, that same Aggie Wilson would right soon gie me the edge o her tongue for interferin wi her business. Aye! She can be a right nippy sweetie that auld woman."

Becky opened her mouth to protest but her mammy wasn't finished yet. "Listen, Becky, Ah micht no hae aw the airs and graces o yer beloved Aunty Meg, but even Ah ken one important fact o life – ye jist hae tae learn tae live and let live. And if truth be telt, Ah'll bet ye a silver sixpence that the Raffertys below us, they–"

Becky broke in: "You mean that couple downstairs with the six children?"

"The very ones. Weel, Ah'm certain sure that mony a time they could see us far enough. Especially when mibbe they've jist got their squad o weans aff tae sleep and they're hopin for a bit o peace and quiet, then oor Erchie gets sterted wi his daft cantrips. Reelin in drunk as a lord, singing his herrt oot about his Granny's Hielan Hame, fallin ower the creepie stool to collapse intae the chair, and droppin his boots fae a great height ontae the flair. Dae ye no think that the Raffertys can hear aw that stramash? Aye, we must be a real trial tae the Rafferty clan, but guid neebors that they are Ah don't recall them iver complainin tae me or iver wance bangin a broom handle on the ceilin neither."

As Becky was finally drifting off to sleep later that evening she smiled to herself. On reflection, between the sounds of screaming children, mewling cats, fighting dogs, scrabbling rats in the back-court middens, the rushing of many waters from the stair-head cludgies, perhaps one squeaking pulley wheel was not after all such a trial. Live and let live.

# Chapter 5

As the weeks passed the two new gophers settled into the job at the carpet factory. The friendship between the girls slowly ripened to the point where not only would they help each other through the hazards, trials and tribulations of each working day, but they would exchange confidences.

Becky raised her head from the task in hand, that of again sweeping a vast expanse of the floor of the mill, to see Caz approaching her with arms over-loaded with heavy bales and her eyes brimming with tears. Close to Becky she indicated a man standing at the far end of the enormous looms by a backward nod of her head.

"Watch oot for that new gaffer. Whitever he tells ye tae dae, dae it bluidy quick. A holy terror that man and English tae boot. Ye can hardly mak oot a word he says."

With that hastily delivered warning Caz hurried on her way leaving Becky in a state of nerves at this new, as yet ill-defined, menace.

When she could not prolong the sweeping of the floor any longer, Becky reluctantly headed towards the end of the room to replace the massive broom in the store cupboard. As she passed the new English gaffer she kept her head down and her eyes averted hoping thus to make herself as inconspicuous as possible.

*After all*, she thought, *no point in looking for extra work or trouble when it can be avoided.*

She turned away from the cupboard and thought she had safely negotiated her way past the gaffer when a shout behind her meant her sigh of relief was premature.

"You girl! Yes, *you.* A word."

Becky looked round and seeing that all other girls within earshot were busy at the gigantic looms with a sinking heart realised the raucous summons must be for her. She trailed her way back to stand in a state of fear and trembling before the giant of a man.

He thrust a paper bag into her hands and barked out the words: "Eat my pie." Then he turned on his heel and marched back to the small enclosure that served as his work area.

Thoroughly bemused by this strange order Becky set off in search of her friend.

*If anyone would know what to do it would be streetwise Caz.*

But luck wasn't with Becky; Caz was nowhere to be found. Becky then remembered that Caz had said she couldn't understand a word the man said, so perhaps Caz wouldn't be much help anyway. Becky on the other hand had had no problem understanding – he had said quite clearly: "Eat my pie."

*Was it some form of initiation joke?* Becky wondered. *Like the time I was sent for a left-handed hammer. Or maybe someone had given the Englishman a Scotch mutton pie and he didn't like it and gave it to me rather than see it wasted.*

With a shrug Becky happily ate the pie as she went about her work. About half-an-hour later a purple-faced gaffer came rampaging through the weaving shed shouting: "Where is that bloody girl? Where the 'ell is she?" When he spotted Becky he bore down on her. "Well, you've taken your time, 'aven't you?"

Becky gaped at him open-mouthed.

"When I tell you to do something, you do it. That's an order and you bloody do it. Got that?"

"Yes, sir."

He pushed his face to within inches of Becky's face. "Well then. So where in God's name is it? Where's my bloody pie? My stomach thinks my throat's cut."

*Where did the stupid man think the pie was?*

When Becky still made no answer the gaffer said: “I asked to you ’eat my pie. Surely that was clear even to your scant intelligence. Stick it on a shovel and warm it over a gas ring.”

Becky felt herself shrivel up inside. This story would haunt her for the rest of her working life in Templeton’s Factory. If her work mates had thought her a stuck-up idiot before, surely this mistake would add fuel to their habitual mockery of her ‘bool in the mooth’ accent.

# Chapter 6

It had been a long hard day in the heat, noise, and frenetic activity of the weaving shed. Now that Becky, having risen from the lowly ranks of being at everyone's beck and call, was now training for the skilled job of tenter the work was becoming daily more arduous and even more physically and mentally exhausting.

Climbing the stairs to her tenement home she was looking forward to a seat at the fireside, a welcoming cup of tea and the promise of a substantial helping of her mammy's mouth-watering stovies to follow. While it was true that despite Becky's ongoing entreaties Mammy still didn't indulge in either the fancy table settings or even the more imaginative varied menus so beloved of Aunt Meg, never-the-less the good plain cooking more than adequately filled the bill.

*Yes*, she thought, *and especially coming in to my evening meal already cooked and waiting for me. I'm certainly a lot luckier than Caz. She has to turn to and prepare and cook the evening meal herself for her idle, lay-about brothers.*

Becky was still mentally counting her blessings as she entered the flat. She was surprised to hear from the kitchen her Aunt Meg's voice. Although Becky visited Meg and Jack's home in the Parliamentary Road weekly, she smiled at the unexpected treat of meeting her at her mother's home. In her haste to hang up her shawl Meg missed not only the hook but the entire rack of hooks and the shawl slithered to the floor. As Becky bent to pick the garment up she froze in mid-motion. Instead of the comfortable drone of polite conversation, what had stopped her was the harsh sound of raised, angry voices issuing from the kitchen.

"Meg, that's enough! Ah'll no hear anither word. Ye and me, we ken fine weel whit we went through. Aye, we baith suffered, so we did. Especially efter yon Hannah Adair telt us you and me could baith end up in bluidy jail if she iver chose tae spill the beans."

Meg's reply, though angry was still ladylike in delivery. "Nellie, I'll thank you to watch your language. I know you're upset by what I've suggested, but even so–"

"Even so, be damned! Becky stays here and let that be the end o it."

Becky, hearing her own name being bandied about, still clutching the shawl drew closer to the closed door.

"Ah suppose it's her bluidy paypoke ye're efter. Ah cannae imagine it's the doubtful pleasure o Becky's company, is it noo?"

A scandalised shout was quickly followed by Aunt Meg's shocked tones. "That's a terrible thing to say, Nellie. Surely you know–"

"Whit a dae ken is this: surely tae heaven Ah'm entitled tae some kind o reward in ma auld age for haen kept up the pretence aw this wheen o years? No much tae ask that, noo is it? For helpin ye tae … for protecting yer guid name."

There seemed to be no reply to this from Meg. Becky pressed her ear even harder against the panel of the door.

"Damnit aw tae hell, Meg, let's face it. If is wisnae for me still keepin ma mooth shut … if Ah wis tae tell the world whit Ah ken there's wan thing sure … if Ah wis tae spill the beans tae yer guid man Jack and aw the rest o the folk roon aboot, ye'd damn sure be drummed oot o aw yon fancy flower-arrangin and ither such ladylike falderals. Aye, yer minister and yon toffee-nosed wife o his, they widnae think ye such a prissy wee goody two shoes then, noo wid they? You a fallen woman wi a bastard child … God Almighty, but the minute they found oot aboot yer daughter Becky–"

At these words, together with an angry shout, there was the sound of a chair being scraped back across the linoleum floor. Realising immediately what this implied, Becky decided to take flight. She flung the shawl she still had in her hand around her shoulders, with trembling fingers turned the brass knob of the hall's outer door, and ran out on the landing pulling the door closed behind her.

She then re-entered the flat noisily, slamming the door behind her and shouting: "Yoo hoo, Mammy, it's only me."

Almost immediately she was face-to-face in the lobby with Aunt Meg as she emerged from the kitchen. Affecting what she fervently hoped was an expression of surprise and pleasure at this unexpected meeting, Becky said: "What a surprise, Aunt Meg, to see you again so soon."

After a quizzical glance at Becky, Meg gave her a perfunctory peck on the cheek and in a voice Becky realised was choked with tears said: "Becky! Sorry I can't stop, dear. I stopped in for a minute to see you're … er … to see my sister. I must rush off now, Jack's expecting me back."

And with that she was off.

This time Becky took her time to hang up her shawl very carefully before she turned towards the kitchen. With her hand on the door handle she wondered if her mammy – *How on earth should she address the woman now? Would her 'mammy' make any reference to what had just passed between herself and her genteel sister?*

# Chapter 7

In the days that followed, Becky found she could not get that overheard conversation out of her head. Should she confront her mammy or her Aunt Meg or perhaps better still both of them? That would require confessing that she had deliberately eavesdropped on their conversation. If the conversation did indeed mean she was the daughter of Aunt Meg should she admit that from the depths of her being she would much rather be the natural, illegitimate daughter of her beloved Aunt Meg than the legally born-in-wedlock daughter of a woman with whom she had nothing in common?

After days of mental anguish Becky was no nearer to making a decision.

A week later walking home from work with Caz, Becky said: "Caz, I need to talk to you – the thing is … my worst nightmare … there's something troubling me."

A look of consternation clouded Caz's face. "Oh, naw, for God's sake, naw! Don't tell me ye're the next tae get caught – like ma sister Lizzy. Ye didnae let that bampot Colin gae aw the wa wi ye efter the last dance?"

Becky felt hot colour rush to her face and was glad the street's dim gas light would help hide her embarrassment from her friend. When she could trust herself to speak Becky said: "Caz! Can you think of nothing else these days? Honestly surely there's more to life than *that*."

Caz stopped and turned to face Becky. "Nae call for ye tae get aw uppity wi me. It's the way o the world. Frae yon randy foreman that's aye chasin efter us lassies tae ivery eejit that thinks he's in wi a fightin chance if he buys us a bag o chips as he walks us hame frae the soirée. See men! Aw the same so they are. Only efter the wan thing."

With a shrug Caz started to walk on, then she stopped again. "Becky, therr is wan thing. Best freens or no if ye've been daft enough tae get caught, ye'd better get a weddin ring on yer finger pretty damn quick for Ah'm no aboot tae help ye wi yer problem. It's agin ma religion."

Becky, now on the verge of a fit of giggles at the turn the conversation had taken, said: "You mean you wouldn't lift a finger to help? Not even with a bottle of cheap gin?"

"Oh Ah'll help ye aw right. Ah'll be yer bridesmaid. Ah'll dance at yer weddin in the Co-op Hall. But onythin mair than that forget it. Efter aw, ye widnae be the first sixteen-year-old bride aw done up in white wi a bairn awready in her belly."

At these words Becky could contain her mirth no longer and as her laughter rang out she held on to the nearest lamppost for support. A passing elderly lady gave her a sour look muttering something about the "evils of drink". This ill-considered, judgemental comment only added to Becky's hysterical mirth. When finally her fit of giggles had subsided and she explained to Caz that far from seeking advice regarding an unwanted pregnancy all she wanted were Caz's views about a family row, Caz too laughed.

"Oh, Becky, a family barney. Is that aw? Forget it, hen. Ma advice is tae leave weel enough alain – jist get on wi yer ain life. But mind ye haud tight tae yer knickers' elastic, yer best freen – at least until yer safely married. And don't forget Ah'm promised for tae be yer bridesmaid."

# Chapter 8

In the few months since Becky's discovery about her parenthood and her decision to follow Caz's advice, "to leave well enough alone," a degree of uneasy peace had descended on the Bryden household. Not that there was any greater feeling, far less any outward display of affection between Becky and her mother and brother but at least they could get through most days without screaming rows.

One morning just as Becky was about to leave for work Nellie said: "Two of yer sisters will be here when ye get hame the nicht – Augustina and Sarah. Ye wouldnae know their weans, of course, ye've niver met them livin away frae Glesga as they dae but they're yer nieces and nephews so ye should get tae know them."

Becky didn't have good memories of any of her four older sisters and the one four years younger than her, Elspeth, had died quite young of diphtheria. After she gone to live with Aunt Meg, visits to Mammy had been a bit of a nightmare. Erchie and the older sisters had made no secret of their jealousy of Becky's better clothes and openly scornful of her, to them, affected speech and manners. However, if she had to meet any of them again Augustina and Sarah were probably the least obnoxious.

After a hard day's work which had included a difficult run-in with one of the new, recently promoted, highly officious gaffers Becky felt tired and out of sorts and wanted nothing more than to get to the flat, have a reviving cup of tea, and soak her feet in a basin of hot water. As she attempted to enter her own close-mouth several children who were having a riotous game of kick-the-can, to the detriment of any passing pedestrians, obstructed her way. Becky weaved first one way then another, but outnumbered as she was could make no progress. When the rusty old can came hurtling towards her shin, in a white heat of anger she lifted her booted foot and dealt the can a hefty kick. This had the effect of scattering the children, allowing her clear passage, but the can found a target in the leg of one of the children. In the ensuing shouted obscenities which followed her, Becky resolutely went on climbing the stairs muttering under her breath: "Perhaps they'll go and play at their own close now and give us a bit of peace and quiet."

Approaching her own door Becky recognised the tempting aroma of clootie dumpling. Ever since she could remember, this Scottish delicacy with its mouth-watering blend of fruits and spices had been Becky's favourite sweet bite. Even so it had been many a long day since she had the good fortune to be the recipient of a large slice.

*Somebody's in for a treat*, she thought. *Just a pity it won't be the Bryden household. Every Scottish housewife regularly turns out a perfect clootie dumpling – but not my mammy.*

However, the moment she entered the flat she was amazed to find that not only was the dumpling to be the *pièce de résistance* after all but that the kitchen table was packed to capacity with other goodies.

Becky was beginning to enjoy being re-acquainted with her older sisters and was beginning to feel that, yes, perhaps it might be pleasant to be part of a large family group when the door bust open to admit a horde of noisy children to disturb the previously quiet domestic scene. One child whose knee dripped blood, took one look at Becky and screamed: "Mammy, that's her! That's the woman that kicked an auld time can at me. Mammy, ma knee – Ah'm dyin. She's a bad woman."

# Chapter 9

In the end it was not Becky who had to have recourse to a hastily arranged marriage. Despite all her warnings and helpful advice on the subject, Caz was the one to find to her utter panic and consternation that she had fallen. In almost less time than it took to tell, Mrs Cassidy, even without a shotgun, had made Declan, the reluctant bridegroom, aware of his imminent, and as far as she was concerned inescapable responsibilities. She had also seen to the wedding details and had obtained from a stall in Paddy's Market a well-used wedding gown which the businesslike dealer had agreed to buy back at a reduced cost the day after it had served its purpose.

At the reception with real sighs of relief from the Cassidy clan there was an air of rejoicing on all sides. In the middle of the hilarity Becky turned to find the best man Ewan at her side.

He smiled down at her and said: "Er … I suppose … I suppose it's traditional … so before Mrs Cassidy tells me off … I'd better ask you since I'm the best man and you're the only bridesmaid … What I mean is … I'd better ask you to have a dance with me."

Becky felt she'd had more gracious invitations to take to the dance floor. Even the more common, but robustly honest, traditional, "Ur ye dancing?" would have been infinitely more acceptable than this hesitant, stuttered, but above all sullen surrender to a hated duty. She frowned and peered through the haze of tobacco smoke at the lanky young man.

"Oh, you poor soul. I'm sorry you've been lumbered with me and such an onerous duty."

Ewan's face flushed and Becky felt a glow of satisfaction that her reply had obviously hit home.

The young man fidgeted with his tie. "I could maybe have put it a wee bit better. But what do you think? Do you fancy tripping the light fantastic with me?"

Becky drew herself to her full height and even then had to look up at him. "Listen, Ewan, or whatever your name is, I wouldn't dance with you even if you were the last man on earth."

With that she strode across the hall to join the newlyweds.

Caz turned to greet her friend. "You're lookin very pleased wi yersel, Becky. And nae wonder. Ah see ye've made a hit wi the best man. A real catch he'd be. He's got a steady job at Fairfields Yard – a draughtsman no less – and they say he's weel connected. His granny owns a couple o wee single ends in Govan."

Becky's scowled. "Caz, just because you're safely wed, don't think you can start lining me up a possible husband and certainly not that ill-mannered lout."

"Becky, surely marriage tae ony decent wage-earnin man wid be better than slavin yer guts oot for the rest o yer life in the carpet mill."

"Decent man did you say? Well, if that's what you call decent and mannerly – if it's all the same to you – I'll take my chances on being left on the shelf and slaving away at Templeton's."

Becky started to turn away to join another group of wedding guests, but Caz grabbed her arm. "Hae it yer own wey. Ah jist hope ye wernae rude tae Ewan. If ye must know, the poor fella is desperate shy. He can hardly look at a woman, far less speak tae her withoot blushin and stammerin."

"If he's that shy, why on earth did Declan have him for his best man? Let's face it, he didn't sound shy or lacking in confidence when he gave his speech."

Caz grinned. "Oh, aye, his best man's speech wis fine. It seems he learnt it aff by hert oot a book in the library. It's jist aroon wimen that he seems tae get aw tongue-tied. Apart frae that he's no at his most sociable the noo, his ither granny – his Brigton granny – died last week. Aye, it says a lot for him that he didnae let us doon at the last minute. Ah hope ye didnae gie the poor chap the benefit o yer high-falutin, hoity-toity lady o the manner shenanigans. He'd be fair terrified o ye, so he would."

# Chapter 10

Penitent and rather embarrassed, Becky slowly made her way back to where Ewan was still standing alone.

"Ewan, I'm sorry I spoke as I did –"

Blushing a furious red, Ewan interrupted her. "No … no, I'm sorry … it was me … I'm very clumsy. It wasn't right the way I said it."

Becky smiled at him. "What say we just pretend it didn't happen and start again? You were right, the best man and the bridesmaid should have a least one dance together. Shall we?"

Certainly not a conversationalist, Ewan went through the whole dance in silence and Becky wondered how with his disadvantage about speaking to girls he managed to become such a practiced dancer. After thanking him for the dance, Becky asked him if would get her a drink and later, sipping the drink, to break the awkward silence, she said: "You're really a very good dancer, Ewan. Where did you learn?"

"You'll laugh," he said.

"No, I won't, I promise."

Ewan shifted from foot to foot. "My older sister taught me. Our folks wouldn't allow her to go to dances on her own, so when I was fifteen she had me go with her. A lot of her pals used to be at the dances and if they didn't have a partner with them they danced with me."

Becky burst out laughing. At the hurt expression on Ewan's face she tried to convert the laugh into a pretend choke on her drink.

"I knew you'd laugh."

"Honest, Ewan, I'm not laughing at you." Becky giggled. "Oh, yes I am. You must admit it's funny. You get tongue-tied talking to girls, asking a girl for a dance, but from fifteen you get girls to dance with without you asking."

"They were all older than me, like my sister, and I only got to dance with them if nobody else asked them."

"You do realise, Ewan, you've said several whole sentences without a stutter or stammer?"

Ewan grinned. "So I have. Maybe we should dance again."

"Not the most elegant invitation," Becky said, "but certainly better than the last."

Blushing again Ewan said: "Sorry, I–"

"I'm joking, Ewan. Let's dance."

Determined this time not to circle the floor in silence, Becky said: "You don't talk like the others."

Ewan missed a step, then recovered. "Neither do you."

"I was brought up by an Aunt who made me learn to speak like this. What about you?"

Again Ewan almost tripped. "My folks were from Inverness originally –"

Becky said: "Oh, yes, I've head that almost everyone there talks what they call posh here."

Ewan lurched again. "Look, I don't think I can dance *and* talk. Do you think we can wait to talk till the dance is over?"

Becky laughed. "Is that an invitation?" Ewan stumbled once more. "Okay, Ewan, you promise to get me another drink after this and talk, and I'll not say another word this dance."

By the time it was announced the newlyweds were leaving, Becky and Ewan had danced together several times and when Becky danced with someone else, Ewan had stood talking with other men.

They were standing together when Caz and Declan turned back to face the guests. Caz, with a grin, threw the small bouquet she was holding straight at Becky who caught it just before any of the other girls got to it. Over her shoulder Caz shouted: "Remember, Ah get tae dance at *yer* weddin."

When the festivities were breaking up Ewan cleared his throat nervously. "Can I walk you home, Becky?"

"It's not all that far, Ewan. We're just on Main Street. Where do you have to go?"

"Govan."

"That's quite a long way."

"I'll get a late tram or I'll walk. I've done that before when I visited my Granny in Bridgeton."

As they left the Co-op Hall, Becky linked arms with Ewan.

With a giggle Becky said: "Can you walk and talk, or is just talking and dancing that's a problem?"

Ewan laughed. "I think I can do both with you. Can I see you again, Becky? There's to be a soirée at our church in Govan, Saturday week. Would you go with me?"

# Chapter 11

Becky did go to the soirée and was relieved to find that Ewan was Protestant like her and not Catholic like Caz. Not that she would have minded, but she felt that Aunt Meg and Uncle Jack might have some reservations about her marrying outside her church. Mammy, Mrs Bryden, probably would have objected, but Becky no longer cared what Mammy would think.

Ewan was fun to be with and he and Becky began to meet regularly once a week. On one occasion when Ewan was walking Becky home they encountered a belligerent, drunken Erchie who blocked their way.

"Excuse us," Ewan said, as he attempted to sidestep Erchie.

"Am Ah no guid enough to meet yer freen?" Erchie said, swaying before them.

Becky shuddered. "Ewan, this is my brother Erchie."

"Pleased to meet you," Ewan said and held out his hand.

"God save us," Erchie said. "Anither bool-in-the-mooth eejit. Could ye no find a proper man tae shack up wi?"

"Don't talk to Becky like that."

"Oh, aye. And who's tae stop me?"

"Just let us past, please."

Erchie made a grab at Becky's arm and Ewan pushed him back.

With a roar Erchie took a wild swing at Ewan who pushed Becky back out of the way, easily avoided Erchie's attempted punch, and then landed two solid punches of his own. The first to

Erchie's midriff made him gasp and bend forward, the second on the point of Erchie's chin rocked him back staggering to bang his head on the wall.

Calmly, Ewan took Becky's arm. "Sorry I pushed you, but I thought you might get hurt."

Becky looked at Erchie slumped against the wall, mumbling incoherently.

"Where did you learn to do that, Ewan? That was great."

Ewan laughed. "I was brought up in Govan. Need I say more? Anyway, working at the shipyard I can't afford to take any guff from anyone. Will you be all right? I mean, he won't try anything when he gets home?"

"No, I'll be fine. The last time he thought he could come the big man I hit him with the frying pan."

"I'll need to keep that in mind in future." Ewan grinned. He walked her up the stairs to her door. "I'll see you next week?"

"Be careful, Ewan, when you go out of the close. Don't turn your back on Erchie. He's got a nasty temper."

"Maybe I should borrow the frying pan? Don't worry, I can look after myself."

Two weeks after Ewan's confrontation with Erchie, Mrs Bryden said to Becky: "Before ye gae oot the nicht just sit yersel doon. We have some talkin tae dae."

Becky sat at the table opposite Mrs Bryden. "Could this not wait till later? I'm going to meet Ewan."

"That's whit we hae tae talk aboot. Erchie telt me aboot how Ewan attacked him for nae reason."

"Oh, that's rubbish, Mammy. Erchie was falling down drunk, as usual, and he was going to hit me before Ewan stopped him."

"Aye, mibbe, but Ah had Erchie find oot something aboot that Ewan. He's frae Govan – a real rough lot there–"

Becky laughed. "And Erchie's pals are all angels?"

"I don't want ye mixin wi the wrang crowd."

"You should have thought of that before you had me working at Templeton's."

"Ah'll have hae nane o that cheek, missie. Ah'm jist thinkin o yer ain guid. Onywey, Ah'll no hae ye thinkin ye can run aff and get married. If Erchie gaes ye'll need tae be here tae look efter yer Mammy and yer Paw – ye owe us that."

Becky stared at Mrs Bryden in disbelief. "You can't stop me getting married."

Mrs Bryden. "Weel, mibbe no directly, but there's some things ye dinnae ken."

"I know you're not my mother. Aunt Meg is. I've gone on pretending I didn't know so as not to embarrass Aunt Meg, but you can't keep me here against my will."

Mrs Bryden gave a sly smile. "Ah did wonder if ye'd overheard Meg and me that day, but when ye didnae let on, Ah thought it best tae leave weel enough alain. Onywey Ah ken yer Ewan's folk are guid church gaein people, even if they dae live in Govan. Whit dae ye think they'll hae tae say if they learn yer a bastard? Think yer Ewan will be sae keen then?"

Becky felt the colour drain from her face. "You would do that to your own sister?"

Grimly, Mrs Bryden said: "Aye, if Ah need tae. Ye can go on seein the lad if ye like, but any hint of ye gettin married and Ah'll put the kibosh on it."

# Chapter 12

In February of 1916 just after the Conscription Act was passed on January 27th Becky and Ewan had been courting for some five months. Becky was afraid that Ewan would be called up for the army but he assured her that as an apprentice draughtsman in a shipyard busy with Admiralty orders he was quite safe unless he volunteered. For Erchie, however, his employment as coal-carrier wasn't considered to be essential to the war effort and by Becky's seventeenth birthday in July he was in uniform. For a few months that followed, Mrs Bryden referred to Ewan as Becky's coward, but Becky refused to rise to the bait and the uneasy truce that had been established between them after the confrontation about Becky's parentage resumed.

The courtship of Becky and Ewan continued sedately. Becky had introduced him to Aunt Meg and Uncle Jack, who had both been suitably impressed, Aunt Meg being particularly pleased with Ewan's lack of a 'coarse Glasgow accent'. Uncle Jack thought Ewan's job in the shipyard drawing office would 'keep his hands clean' and ensure good steady work. The two year gap in their ages was 'just right'.

In May of 1918 a strange new influenza appeared in Glasgow – the Spanish Flu that had been affecting troops at the front in France since early spring – and there were reports of many people taking ill. As had been the case with the plague outbreak in 1900, Meg was very concerned and talked at length to Becky about precautions she should take. However, it was Rab who was struck down and by June was dead. Ewan was puzzled and a little concerned at how calmly Becky took the sad news of the death of her father.

Caz, at one of Becky's visits, quizzed Becky about Ewan. "Ye've been courtin for mair than two years now. Is it no time he popped the question? Yer no gettin ony younger. Yer, whit, nineteen noo?"

Becky sighed. "We're fine as we are. Apart from Erchie and he's as much use as a sore head, Mammy has no one to bring any money into the house now that my father's dead."

"As far as Ah could make oot yer faither didnae bring anythin but booze intae the hoose while he *was* alive."

"Ewan understands. We'll just have to wait a while. Maybe when Erchie comes back from the war he'll be more sensible ..."

"Aye, and then he'll get himself hitched and ye'll still be left the spinster sister tae look efter auld maw. Ah tell ye. Ah ken. That's how it is wi ma younger sister."

"Just drop it, Caz. Let's talk about something else."

Caz's repeated comments began to irritate Becky and she stopped visiting her, but Caz's reference to Becky ending up a spinster-of-the-Parish rankled and her resentment against Mammy built steadily.

One day at work when the machines were down for a spell Becky overheard two of the girls talking. One was explaining to the other that since she was marrying a Catholic and having to convert, the priest wanted to see her birth certificate.

"Well," she said, "wouldn't ye know but ma certificate got lost in one of oor moonlights."

The other laughed. "Aye, a flittin jist steps ahead o the bailiffs can be a bit rushed. Easy tae lose things. But ye can get a copy o yer certificate frae the Registrar's Office. It'll cost ye though."

The machines started up again and Becky spent the afternoon thinking about the conversation she'd just heard.

Two weeks later, after the evening meal Becky turned to her mammy.

"Would you still tell everyone about me being Aunt Meg's daughter and not yours if I decided to get married?"

"Ah don't think Ah'll hae tae tell, will Ah? Ah wid bet ye'd dae onythin no tae upset yer precious Aunt Meg." Mrs Bryden sat back with a self-satisfied smirk on her face.

"You've bet on the wrong horse, this time, *Mammy*. Last week I managed to get time off from the mill–"

"That's the week yer paypoke wis some hours short! Ye lyin wee bisom! Ye telt me some machine broke doon and ye were aw short."

"Right. I went to the Registrar's Office. Did you know you can get a copy of your birth certificate? I've got one. It says quite clearly: 'Becky Bryden, Daughter of Rab Bryden and Nellie Bryden', and it's signed by Nellie Bryden. If you try to tell anyone anything else without some witness to the contrary, you'll just be a crazy old woman. If the Registrar did believe you, who would be in bother for signing an official document to a lie? As for trying anything else to keep me at home to look after you – slavery was abolished years ago, *Mammy*. Now, I'm going out to meet Ewan."

On Becky's twenty-fifth birthday Ewan's proposal was finally accepted and on St Valentine's Day, 1925 they were married. Ewan's Govan granny gave one of her single ends – just vacated – rent free as a wedding present. Mrs Bryden reluctantly attended the wedding and the reception in the Co-op Hall, which was paid for by Aunt Meg and Uncle Jack. Caz did get to dance at Becky's wedding, albeit somewhat awkwardly being heavy with her fourth child.

In December 1928, following an entire day and night of hideous pain during which Becky prayed for the release of an early death, baby Val finally came into the world. Ewan and the assortment of relatives and friends who came to gaze at and admire the couple's first baby all marvelled at the fact that the baby had been born on the shortest day of the year. Becky felt she could well have taken issue with this, for as far as she was concerned, far from being the shortest day it had been the longest, dreariest, most ghastly day of her entire life to date. She also silently vowed – never again!

*How other women of her acquaintance could produce a child every year of marriage and still come smiling though life,* Becky thought, *is a complete mystery to me. I'll certainly steer clear of becoming such a baby factory.*

How she would achieve such a miracle was not entirely clear. However, now that the baby was safely born Becky felt her world was complete. She had her own good man, a husband who, unlike many in Govan, brought home to her, unopened, a weekly pay-packet from the yard. Now she had a bonnie baby to love, to care for, and to dress-up like a wee doll.

*Yes*, Becky thought, *it's all a far cry from living with* Mammy's *perpetual complaints about me not doing enough for her and her lay-about Rab who would neither work nor want.* She smiled. *It's even further from the stress, hellish noise and frenetic activity of the carpet factory.*

As she looked round her home from the comfort of her chair, almost as if taking stock for the first time, she saw the centre of her world in the polished-for-dear-life black range with its overhanging gas mantle, the mantle with her wally dugs, brass candlesticks, tea caddy, and the mantle clock.

Her gaze fell on the recessed wall-bed with its patchwork quilt, the marital bed in which baby Val had been joyfully conceived and later brought into the world. As she cradled the baby in her arms, Becky vowed she would bring up her child to become a decent citizen and far removed from the appearance, manners, and slovenly speech of the archetypical *Glesga Keelie.*

To this end, Becky, rather than relying on any innate maternal instincts took to spending hours on end in the nearby Elder Park Library perusing volumes on childrearing.

# Chapter 13

Aunt Meg and Uncle Jack had just left to catch a tram to Parliamentary Road when Becky rounded on Ewan.

"What was wrong with you tonight? You hardly said a word the whole tea-time. You barely answered when Uncle Jack tried to tease you about your football team losing again. It was downright rude of you."

Ewan nodded. "I know. I'm sorry. I just have a lot on my mind."

"It had better be something pretty important to justify your behaviour tonight."

"It is. I didn't want to tell you before Aunt Meg arrived and spoil their visit but … that pay-packet I gave you last night … it could be a long time before we see another one. I told you things were deadly quiet at Fairfields. I've been lucky till now … but I was in the last batch to be paid off. The yards are closing all up and down the Clyde there'll be no jobs for draftsmen anywhere."

Two months later, just a month short of Val's third birthday there was an addition to the family. Sadly for a hopeful Val this was not the longed-for kitten or puppy, or even a budgerigar or goldfish about which she had been harping on ever since she could string two words together. No, the arrival came in the form of a red-faced, squalling, squirming bundle all happed up in a white knitted shawl. When Val questioned this mystery, she learned that Becky had found the bundle under a gooseberry bush and had, stupidly in Val's opinion, elected to bring it home to join their family.

Val's question as to why her mother couldn't have looked for a gooseberry bush that had kittens instead of a baby only produced puzzling gales of laughter and her query on what exactly was a gooseberry bush and which back court it was to be found in reduced her parents to fits of giggles.

A little later when Val's dark feelings of sibling rivalry and jealousy erupted into surreptitious nipping of the baby and deliberate acts of petty vandalism on Scott's few precious toys, Becky again resorted to the volumes at the Elder Park Library.

A study of the latest books on new-fangled child psychology informed Becky that the best way to avoid or at least modify sibling rivalry was to make the child feel useful. This revolutionary idea was that the useful child would soon realise she was an important, vital, highly-valued member of the new domestic set-up and the behaviour of the previously jealous child would miraculously change.

Desperate to try anything, Becky immediately put this gem of wisdom into operation in many guises. With the baby on her knee she would smile at Val and say: "Val, I'm going to give the baby his bath now. Can you please bring over his sponge?" Perhaps it was the novelty of the approach which did indeed seem to work. Toddler Val, a willing slave bursting with self-importance, trotted to and fro in the single end with the never-ending list of nappies, towels, dusting powder and jars of nappy-rash cream.

*Yes*, thought Becky, *the books were right. Val's behaviour has changed.*

Unfortunately, after a very short time the previously sneaky attacks became not only more frequent but more ferocious. She rebelled at being a slave-in-waiting for the baby's every need and demonstrated this by throwing herself on the floor in temper tantrums, developing a stutter, and, when all her other tactics failed, resorted to wetting the bed.

Becky, at her wit's end, discussed the matter with Caz on one of her visits to Govan.

Caz, by now the mother of four bairns and heavy with a fifth, grinned at Becky. "Whit wiz it ye were studyin at the library? Whit did ye cry it? Piss-ology somethin or other?"

Becky smiled. "Nearly right, Caz, Psychology, Child Psychology. According to it, if you go the right way about it, you can bring up any child to go the way you want. It's all very simple really."

"Simple, ye say? Aye, simple's the word. Let's face it, hen, if ye want yer wee girl tae grow up as a nasty piece o goods, stutterin and peein at will aw ower the shop, as weel as rampagin aw ower everythin belangin tae other folk – aye, fine. Yer gaein the right wey aboot it."

Becky, inwardly seething and hurt to the core by Caz's outburst, simply said: "Trust you, Caz – you always go right to the heart of a problem, don't you?"

"Ah've had plenty o practice. Ye name it – onythin frae fractious, vomiting weans tae Friday nicht wife-batterin men, randy wi it – Ah'm the authority. If ye really want ma advice ..."

Becky nodded.

"It's like this, hen, forget aw aboot aw that book learnin. If yer Val is being naughty, a guid whack tae her bare bahoochie will work wonders. In ma estimation nae bairn wi a sair, skelpit bum iver dun the same mistake twice."

Staring at her friend in disbelief Becky started to protest, But Caz would have none of it.

"It's a bluidy true sayin – spare the rod and spoil the child. And by the time ye've got half a dozen weans ..."

Becky shuddered. "Half-a-dozen temper-tantrum Vals. Perish the thought."

# Chapter 14

Ewan's parents, Tibby and Andrew Graham, lived on Crossloan Road and with this being so close to Becky's single end on Langlands Road there was naturally much coming and going between the two households. Ever since the births of Val and her brother Scott the elderly couple revelled in their status as grandparents and would answer only to the names of Grampa and Gramy Graham.

Hardly a day would pass without Val saying: "Mammy, can we go round to see Grampa and Gramy Graham after school?"

Becky thus got into the habit of meeting Val at the school gate at three o'clock and pushing Scott's go-chair between them, the pair would arrive in time for afternoon tea. Grampa Graham who worked on permanent night-shift as the Night Supervisor for Glasgow Corporation Cleansing Department, by three-thirty would be up from his sleep, washed, and dressed in his off-duty finery.

*The Cleansing,* as Becky discovered when she first met Ewan's parents, was the polite term for the midgie-men who emptied the middens during the night and transported the rubbish to the destructor on Craigton Road where Mr Graham worked. There the rubbish was sorted into various categories and the combustibles burned.

Becky would also never forget her first sight of Mr Graham – she had never before seen such an eccentric or bizarre style of dressing. For his hours of relaxation at home, like the laird of some country estate, he wore a red velvet smoking jacket, fine moleskin trousers, and, to top his outfit off, a matching red velvet smoking hat with a long silver tassel, the strands of which waved elegantly to and fro as he spoke.

Ewan later confided to Becky that the jacket and hat were *perks* of his father's position as Night Supervisor and that: "It's amazing what some of the posh West End folk throw out."

With his precious wee grandson on his knee there surely wasn't a happier man in the entire Second City of the Empire than Grampa Graham as the toddler played endlessly with the fascinating silver tassel.

# Chapter 15

As the months passed Ewan despaired of getting any paid work. Uncle Jack at the bank had nothing he could offer and although Grampa Graham could possibly have pulled some strings, the only work he could have found for Ewan was as one of the midgie-men as, Depression or not, the Cleansing Department still had to work. This dirty, unpleasant but essential job, cleaning out the city's middens, was also very hard physical labour and, at thirty-seven, Ewan's years of sitting or standing drawing in the shipyard hadn't prepared him for this type of exertion. Although he was willing to try, Grampa Graham ruled out the option.

Becky, in an effort to comfort Ewan, only succeeded in driving him further into despair when she pointed out that they were luckier than most, since both Uncle Jack and Grampa Graham were still fully employed and were more than willing and able to help out financially.

After four months of unemployment and hating accepting handouts from his parents and Uncle Jack, Ewan finally walked into the Langlands Road single end with a smile on his face.

"I don't suppose you could teach me to make Scotch broth between now and Monday morning, could you, Becky?" He placed a package with half-a-dozen Scotch mutton pies on the table.

Becky looked at the pies and then in puzzlement at her husband.

"What on earth are you up to?"

Ewan laughed. "I was walking down Elder Street and at that

workman's restaurant just up from Govan Road, I bumped into this chap who was standing on the pavement staring up at the shop front. I said I was sorry, but he laughed. He was looking at his sign. The sign writer who'd been doing it for him had fallen off his ladder and hurt his wrist so the sign was left half done.

"I said I was a draftsman and could fix it up for him. So we went into the shop and he made us a cup of tea ..."

"Okay, fine, but what does all this have to do with making Scotch broth?"

"I'm coming to that. The owner, Alex, had only bought the restaurant before the yards started to slow down then close, so for a while he thought he was going to have to close too. But he now does a roaring trade in carry-out – broth, mince and tatties, pies and gravy, you name it he sells it."

"Ewan I'm going to clout you with the frying pan if you don't come to the point – the Scotch broth."

"Oh, yes, he needs someone to work in kitchen with him. I told him I was a dab hand with broth."

"Ewan, how could you? That's a downright lie."

"Lie be damned, Becky. But I do admit, I neglected to say I was a dab hand at eating it, not making it. I'm sure I can learn."

"What has all this to do with the sign? I thought you were going to tell me you had a job as a sign writer."

"Oh, while we were supping our tea the sign writer laddie came back and said his apprentice would finish the sign in the morning. Alex said I could start work in the kitchen on Monday at seven sharp."

# Chapter 16

Becky chewed at her lower lip as she gazed down at her restlessly sleeping son, and wondered what on earth she should do for the best. Like all other mothers and grannies in the tenements all around her Becky was something of an expert in the myriad of tried and tested home-made cures for just about everything from a sore throat to housemaid's knee. Although she had already fed Scott with the recommended butter-balls rolled in sugar and he now sported an old sock filled with heated salt round his neck and a vinegar-soaked rag on his forehead, he was still no better.

*In fact*, Becky thought, *I have to admit, if anything, the wee lamb seems worse that he did earlier this morning.*

With Ewan now off to work and Val safely packed off to school, Becky had more time to concentrate, worry, and fuss over her ailing son. It was almost unheard-of in their neighbourhood to send for a doctor unless actually facing the jaws of death. Becky, in a dither of indecision, agonised over the best course of action. Eventually, feeling herself to be almost at the screaming point with worry, she decided to talk to the neighbour across the landing.

*If anyone knows what to do*, Becky thought, *Granny MacAlistair should. By all accounts she's brought up a squad of her own bairns. She probably knows more about childhood ailments then any qualified doctor.*

Just minutes after she rattled on the brass lion's head on Granny MacAlistair's door, the old woman examined Scott. She shook her head.

"That wean needs a wheen mair treatment than vinegar rags. He needs a doctor. Ah'll wait here wi him and ye, Becky, fling on yer shawl and scoot doon the road tae get the doctor."

Three-quarters of an hour later Becky closed the door behind the doctor. She stood with her forehead pressed against the rough wood of the lintel. She stared down at her fists clutching the door knob, the knuckles showing white.

*Diphtheria! Mammy's last child – the reason why I went to live with Aunt Meg – died of diphtheria at just about the same age as Scott.*

Granny MacAlistair pried Meg's fingers from the doorknob and led her to sit in the chair beside the fire.

"They'll no be lang, lass, the doctor said. The men should be here ony minute tae take the wee mite away."

"Away, Granny Mac, where? In God's name, where?"

"Tae the fever hospital. Ye don't want yer wee lass, Val, tae catch it tae."

At a loud knock on the door Granny MacAlistair, arthritic or not, leapt to her feet to admit two men carrying two long poles wrapped round with canvas. One of the men had a blanket draped over his arm. The brilliant colour of the wool stood out in sharp red contrast with the dark blue of his uniform sleeve. As the blanket-bearing man approached the bed, the other man whispered some words – presumably words of comfort – to Becky but not one word penetrated through Becky's current living hell.

The man at the bed smiled at Becky then said to his colleague: "It's no a stretcher job this, Jimmy. We'll manage just fine wi the blanket alone. The poor wee mite wid be lost, like a pea in a dumpling, if we wis tae put him on the stretcher."

The ambulance men bent down and with gentle, careful movements peeled back the patchwork quilt. With great tenderness they lifted Scott and wrapped him in the red hospital blanket. When all that could be seen of her son was the mop of damp, disarranged curls, Becky stretched out her hand for one last fond touch of his silken hair.

At a nod from the man carrying Scott the other moved to the door and said: "Right, that's us, Missus. If ye've ony other weans they'll need tae be kept aff the school. Yer hoose will need tae be fumigated and aw library books will need tae be burnt. That's the law, hen."

As if moving in a dream, Becky followed the men through the close as they headed towards the fever van. Just before climbing in, one of the men said: "Yer wee laddie will be at the Fever Hospital, Missus. Although ye'll no be able tae visit him in the actual ward ye can probably get permission – once he's a bit better like, tae hae a wee keek through the window at him."

Becky allowed herself to be led back to her house for the ritual reviving cup of tea. Neither of them voiced the unspoken thought that with diphtheria it might be many a long day, if ever, before they saw Scott again.

Happily, Scott survived the bout with diphtheria and two years later was ready for his first day at school.

# Chapter 17

Becky could not believe how quickly the years were passing. On remarking on this aspect of life to her neighbour across the landing, old Mrs MacAlistair said: "Ah windae worry ower much aboot it, hen, it happens tae aw o us. They say it's a sign o advancin age when ye start tae find years fleein by and ivery month seems mair like a day."

Becky laughed. "Advancing years, you say, Mrs MacAlistair? At thirty-seven I'm not quite decrepit yet, you know."

"Onywey ye care tae look at it, at thirty-seven and the mither o twa weans yer life is ower. Ye've tae see tae yer family. So advancin age is aw that's left tae ye – mibbe between whiles another couple o weans in yer belly afore yer past it."

A week later Becky awoke to the fact that it seemed only yesterday Scott was a shawl-wrapped babe-in-arms yet today there he was standing before her as the latest entrant to Greenfield School. As if awaking from a deep sleep Becky looked in wonder at her son. Yes, there he was: face scrubbed almost raw, his unruly curls plastered down with an illicit handful of his daddy's precious Brylcreem, his wee spindly legs encased in short trousers and his feet in the regulation tackety boots – boots more suited to an Irish navvy than to a puny five-year-old.

She fastened his school bag on his back and turned to her first-born. "Mind now, keep Scott tight by the hand till you deliver him safely to the infant mistress, Miss McQuarry, a lovely lady. He's already been registered so she's expecting him. I'll come up at break and feed a wee sweet bite through the railings to the wee pet."

Val's lips tightened at these words and Becky, realising her mistake, hurried on: "And a little something for you as well, as usual, Val. You know I wouldn't leave you out."

The rest of that morning until break time Becky went about her housework in something of a daze. She agonised over whether or not she had been wise to leave Scott in the not-so-tender mercies of his big sister. Should she herself have gone with him and seen him to the school gates or was it better after all in the long run to give Val this further measure of responsibility in the ongoing battle of sibling jealousy and rivalry?

Becky frowned as she recalled how the curse had again raised its ugly head.

As part of the grand pre-school preparations Gramy and Grampa Graham had appeared on the Saturday before the big day with a selection of gifts. There was: a fully loaded wooden pencil case with a swivelling out tray, a garish design on the lid and the name 'Scott' engraved in pokerwork; a multi-coloured sweater which Gramy had lovingly made with odd bits of wool; and the *pièce de résistance*, a real leather school bag the weight of which would have brought a grown man to his knees.

Far from being delighted with these gifts, Becky had chewed her lower lip in distress at all this largesse bestowed on her son – especially when she caught sight of the look on Val's face.

Gramy Graham handed Val a stick of barley sugar. "This is for you, Val. We didn't want to leave you out, but don't forget when it was your turn to start school you got lots of nice things too."

Eight-year-old Val remembered. She had hated on sight the little cardboard attaché case: the hand-knitted mitts attached by a cord, to thread through her jacket sleeves in case of loss; and most of all she had loathed the gymslip, bought 'for her growth' with its adjustable shoulder strap buttons, made of scratchy serge material which left her thighs red-raw in the cold winter. That detested gymslip was still with her in Primary Three and suitably sponged with a vinegar rag and pleats pressed to razor sharpness every Sunday would doubtless be with her till the end of her primary school days.

Val eyed greedily the spoils bestowed on Scott and after automatically accepting the proffered barley sugar stick she took one look at it and hurled it from her with a howl of protest. The offending sweetie bounced off the wooden mantle-piece then shattered into a thousand glistening pieces on the hearth below.

The afternoon ended in a hurried departure by the doting grandparents; a tearful Scott picking slivers of barley sugar from his sweater where it lay on the chair beside the fireplace; and a screaming-her-head-off Val unable to sit with any degree of comfort on her stinging bare bottom.

*So much for the pre-school celebrations,* Becky thought as she brought her mind back to the present. One glance at the mantelshelf clock told her it was time she was on her way round the corner to Elderpark Street and on up to Greenfield School. She made it just in time. The bell tolled as a breathless Becky joined the other over-anxious mothers standing on the street side of the railings. Like feeding time at the zoo, the mothers stood with jammy pieces in hand ready to thrust through the bars to be snatched by their supposedly starving children. Of Becky's own two, Scott was the first to appear, but rather than eagerly putting out his hand for the bit of buttered gingerbread he seemed strangely withdrawn and tearful. He gazed imploringly at his mother with the words: "Mammy, I want to go home. I don't like school. Don't leave me, Mammy."

Other mothers nearby smile sympathetically and encouraged Scott and Becky.

"Uch, the wee darling – his first day at school?"

"Don't worry, hen. Ma three wus the same their first day – hated it, but look at them noo."

Becky did look and saw a rampaging mob terrorising other children and leading them into mischief.

"Scott, don't worry, son. You'll be fine. When Val brings you home at dinnertime I'll have your favourite – mince and mashed potatoes. You'll like that won't you?"

But Scott would have none of this. All he wanted was home away from this terrible place called school.

As Becky worried about what to do the janitor appeared. When he tolled the mighty school bell, like a well trained army of midgets, the youngsters, all except a now screaming Scott, ran immediately to get to their designated class lines before the redoubtable Miss McQuarry would appear on the scene.

On her arrival, at one glance she caught the sight of one solitary miscreant child hanging on for dear life to the railings and far from the military precision of the ordered class lines. Leaving the janitor to start off the marching, the necessary music already issuing from the piano in the central hall, Miss McQuarry strode purposefully across the playground. She looked through the railings at Becky and said: "We've had trouble with this one already this morning. He gave his sister a real showing up."

Becky wondering what on earth Scott could have done to blot his copy book on his very first morning at school started to ask Miss McQuarry for details, but Miss McQuarry was finished with the mother.

"Right, young man, that's your mother off home. So let's have no more of your nonsense. Peel yourself away from those railings. Inside with you or you'll be at the receiving end yet again for a well earned punishment."

# Chapter 18

The Infant Mistress, despite Becky describing her to Val as a 'lovely lady' earlier, had a well deserved reputation as a strict disciplinarian, terrifying children and parents alike.

By the time Becky arrived home after the morning break, she was hot and flustered. She didn't remember being this worried about Val's first day. Somehow Scott seemed more fragile than Val. She worked herself into such a state that instead of shopping for anything for the children's mid-day meal she made endless cups of hot, sweet tea in an effort to calm her twanging nerves.

*For once in their lives*, Becky thought, *they'll have to make do with just jammy pieces for dinner.*

One look at Scott when the children returned at mid-day was enough to confirm Becky's worst fears. The wee lad, still resplendent in his Joseph's Coat slipover, new short trousers, and brave, tackety boots, never-the-less presented a sorry sight. His good white shirt was hanging awry beneath his pullover, and one top-hose was wrinkled at a rather jaunty angle halfway down his skinny leg. His crowning glory, which Becky had spent hours coaxing into waves and curls, now resembled nothing so much as a bird's nest.

Worst of all, his normally lovely sea-blue eyes were red from weeping and his chubby cheeks tear-stained.

As Becky wiped Scott's nose she could not help noticing the contrast between him and his rather smug-looking sister. Far from taking part in the ongoing domestic drama she had assumed the air of a detached, wary, but only slightly interested bystander. At the moment Becky was aware of an almost overwhelming urge to smack her first-born soundly on her bare bottom for no other reason than the self-satisfied, smug look on her face as she watched her wriggling brother being cleaned up.

Eventually with a still sniffling Scott toying with his jammy piece Becky turned to Val.

"Now, young lady, there'll be no jammy piece for you until you give me a full account of this morning's events. Don't forget, I put you in full charge of your wee brother."

Val sat up straight in her chair. "It wasn't my fault, Mammy. I put him in the right line in the playground. I even waited with him as long as I dared before I ran to my own line with my pals."

Becky looked long and hard at Val especially when Val said: "Don't blame me, Mammy. I done what you asked. Now can Ah get something to eat?"

Aware she was losing the ongoing battle to teach her children to speak properly Becky said: "You *did* what was asked, Val, not *done*. Honestly, girl, will you never learn?"

Hearing this, Scott under the mistaken belief that since Val was now getting a row his own personal crisis was over, stopped sniffling and quite happily started licking the jam from his fingers. Val, as yet unfed, was not about to see the wee pest get off so lightly.

"Mammy, it was his own fault he got the belt. He was cheeky to the teacher."

"Cheeky? Scott, the best behaved boy in Govan, cheeky? Certainly not to Miss McQuarry."

With his halo now firmly in place, Scott smiled his angelic charm.

"I wasn't cheeky, Mammy. I just did what Val told me. I sat up straight at my desk, folded my arms, and …"

As his words trailed off, Val shot him a warning look before he could say more.

"Nothing wrong with that, sonny. What Val told you was fine.

That's how all good pupils behave. But listen, did Val give you any other advice – tell you anything else?"

A nod from Scott and a murderous look from Val prompted a further question from Becky. "So! There *was* something else?"

Scott nodded again. "She told me the right way to answer when the teacher called the roll. Told me to get it right to make a good impression."

"Well, you certainly seemed to have made an impression – but it doesn't seem to have been the right one does it, if you got the strap?"

"Mammy, when the teacher called my name I just said what Val had told me. We practised yesterday. I said: 'Aye, Missus, Ah'm richt here.'"

Becky gasped. "You said what? Scott, my wee darling, you know must always speak properly in school. Rightly or wrongly no child is allowed to speak Broad Scots or the Glasgow dialect in school – it's one language for the street and playground and King's English for the classroom. No wonder you got the belt."

Silence greeted this and as Val tried to slink out the door Becky grabbed hold of her.

"As for you, madam – this is all your fault. Just you wait till your father gets home tonight."

# Chapter 19

When Becky next popped round to see Gramy Graham she made sure she went alone so she could tell the story of Scott's first day without the children listening to every word.

"Poor wee darling," Gramy Graham said. "Mind you, before they're finished with school they'll both get many a sore hand from the teacher's Lochgelly. I can't say it has done Ewan any harm."

Becky grinned. "Is that so? Well, it might have made him a biddable pupil, but I can't say I've noticed him toeing the line as a well-trained husband."

The two women laughed.

"A biddable Scottish husband?" Gramy Graham said. "There's no such creature – unless he's been totally henpecked into submission by which time he's not a man at all, Scottish or otherwise."

They chatted for a time on other matters before Gramy Graham said: "Mind you, I'm sorry Ewan had to chastise Val. I don't think for one minute she meant for any harm to come to her wee brother."

Becky had her own opinion on this overly generous humanitarian theory, but rather than voice it and risk offending her mother-in-law she simply said: "Good of you to say so, but what makes you think that? After all, she can be a real wee madam at times."

Gramy Graham smiled fondly. "Oh, it's just her way. She's the drama queen of this family. Just like Ewan's sister. Anyway, I do know that she loves the old Scots tongue, so I expect it just slipped out unawares in all the excitement of giving Scott his orders and telling him to mind his P's and Q's."

"As to her being a drama queen, she's all that and more. But I don't quite get your drift about her love of the old Scots language. She doesn't hear it spoken at home, and the accent you and Grampa Graham have is far removed from the coarse way the people round here speak."

"No secret there, Becky. I know you're fussy about her speaking proper English but any time she's here on her own there's nothing she likes better than to hear Grampa quote some of the old Scottish weaver poets."

Becky raised her eyebrows and Gramy Graham went on: "She really loves them. I think her favourite is *Drucken Tam the Baker*. Although when I come to think of it she's really daft about a poem by a lad called Nicholson, *Imph-m, that awfy word imph-m.*"

Gramy Graham closed her eyes then quoted:

"Ye've heard hoo the deil, as he wauchel'd through Beith,
Wi' a wife in ilk oxter and ane in his teeth,
When someone cried oot, 'Will ye tak' mine the morn?'
He wagged his auld tail while he cocked his horn,
But only said Imph-m! That useful word Imph-m,
Wi' sic' a big mouthfu' he couldna say, aye!"

Becky laughed. "Yes, I could see that one amusing Val, considering the number of times I've told her not to say, imph-m, instead of the proper, yes. However, poetry and performing is one thing, she still has to learn to speak properly when appropriate."

On her way home Becky remained unconvinced about the supposed innocence of Val's instruction to Scott, but the conversation had convinced her that as soon as she could scrape together enough money Val should have elocution lessons. Aunt Meg had done as much for her and she could do no less for Val.

# Chapter 20

Becky knew that had Ewan still been unemployed there would not have been a hope of managing to save the requisite half-crowns far less put her grand plan into operation. But Ewan had been happily employed in the restaurant for over five years and although the pay wasn't tremendous he had a steady pay-packet and in addition he brought home generous helpings of stale pies and odds and ends of food left over at the end of the day which would not keep for the next.

Finally after months of slipping the odd few coppers at a time into the tea caddy Becky had no less than three half-crowns. With the money safely tucked in her purse she set out in pursuit of the one person she knew could help her. Leaving the children in the charge of Gramy Graham, Becky walked round the corner to Craigton Road to catch the yellow tram which would take her back to Bridgeton. For most of the journey she sat lost in her dreams, but the sight of Templeton's Carpet Factory with its extravagant palazzo-style frontage made her think of the years she had worked there – the long hard years toiling, paying her money every week to Mammy until she had the courage to finally confront her and escape to marry Ewan. Becky shivered. The present even with the Depression was much to be preferred.

The woman she was intent on visiting, Becky hoped, still lived in a tenement near the People's Palace. Even when she had been Becky's elocution teacher all those years ago Abigail Andrews had been almost crippled with arthritis and had seldom strayed far from her home where she looked after her aged mother.

Arriving out of breath at the top floor flat, Becky tugged at the brass bell pull.

*I'd forgotten that staircase,* Becky thought. *Of course I was just a child then. How on earth, does poor Abigail on her infrequent sojourns into the world manage with that winding, heart-stopping stair which seems to reach skyward for ever?*

After a short wait, Becky tried the bell pull again. She could hear the *ting* of the bell echoing through the hall beyond the door. Then she could hear a voice muttering something she didn't catch as it approached.

The door opened and a withered old prune of a woman walking with two sticks peered out at Becky.

*Her mother?* Becky thought. *That's how I remember her mother. But that's more than twenty years ago.*

Coming to her senses Becky, as though addressing someone of an elevated social strata far above her own humble origins, said: "Miss Andrews? Please do forgive my arriving unannounced in this way but …"

The old lady with a joyous cry of greeting dropped her sticks and enveloped Becky in a hug. They stood locked in this embrace for several minutes before at last Abigail clutching both of Becky's arms pushed them a little apart.

"Becky Bryden! Becky is it really you?"

Somewhat dazed by this unexpected rapturous welcome Becky mumbled: "Yes, Miss Andrews, none other."

Becky helped Abigail pick up her walking sticks and they moved to the parlour.

"You've changed, Becky. Grown into a handsome young woman … and married … with two children I hear. A far cry from the fourteen year-old I last saw. But I would have recognised your voice anywhere."

Becky felt close to tears. "You said you'd heard about me? How …?"

"Your Aunt Meg's church and mine occasionally have functions in common and I bump into her from time to time. When I do I always ask after you. You were my star and favourite pupil. You could have gone on to greater things."

"What exactly do you mean, Miss Andrews?"

Abigail smiled kindly, as at a not-too-bright child. "With your personality, your drive, your beautiful vowels – you could easily have become a famous actress. I expected at least you would have gone on to study and become a teacher. Quite the most promising of all my students. Of course, I understand you had no choice but to go back to your mother when she needed you. But still a great loss."

With a rueful smile Becky said: "The beautiful vowels were thanks to your expert tuition – and of course to Aunt Meg paying for my lessons. Alas, they didn't do me much good working in Templeton's Carpet Factory … but that's in the past." Becky paused, aware of and now embarrassed about the twenty-three year lapse in time since she had last visited Miss Andrews. "I really must apologise for not having been in touch with you before – I was just a child of fourteen when I went back to live with my mother … it was an upsetting time and I was angry and confused … my speech was so unlike that of others around me that I suppose I resented the difference and … maybe blamed both you and Aunt Meg for it … and by the time I got over that …"

"Life went on?" Abigail smiled. "As you say, that's all in the past and there's nothing we can do about it. You're here now, and I assume not simply to reminisce …"

"Do you still teach?"

"Yes, I may look more decrepit than you remember – none of us is getting any younger – but I'm only sixty."

*That means when I last saw her,* Becky thought, *she must have been the same age as I am now, thirty-seven.*

"I have a real little drama queen in my family, my eight year-old Val, and she is the reason I have come to see you today."

"Right, Becky, if you'd like to help me, I think we should have some tea over which you can tell me all your news and about little Val. We can also discuss arrangements for lessons."

# Chapter 21

Throughout the rest of that autumn and well into the cold days of the winter every Saturday afternoon without fail Becky left Scott with his adoring Gramy Graham and she and Val took the yellow tram to Bridgeton. Ostensibly, the journeys were to see Caz and her family but, of course, the hour of tuition with Miss Andrews was paramount.

Towards the end of November, Abigail took Becky aside. "I am really pleased with the progress Val has made. With your permission, of course, I've decided to enter her for a poetry reading competition."

Becky's eyes widened in amazement. "I can hardly believe that. She must be really good – for when *I* was your pupil you never entered *me* for any elocution exams or competitions."

With a mischievous gleam in her eye Abigail tapped Becky's arm. "No need to fish for compliments, Becky. The opportunity somehow never arose in your case. But this is different."

"Different? In what way different?"

"Let's just say, then I didn't have the useful contacts I have now. But the thing is, what do you think of the idea? I do hope you'll agree – in any case I've already been teaching Val the test piece, so it would certainly be shame to waste all that effort wouldn't it?"

Becky didn't need to give the matter a second thought, so gratified was she at the very though of her daughter being considered sufficiently skilled in proper speaking to be entered in an elocution contest.

The evening of the contest finally came. In a small draughty hall in Partick's Dumbarton Road a group of sixty would-be elocutionists gathered, each with a band of supporters, braving the January weather. For Val, Becky had dragooned Grampa and Gramy Graham, assorted friends, schoolmates, and some church members into attending. They arrived early, saving a seat for Abigail while Val trooped off backstage to join the other hopefuls and have a last practice at her soon to be publicly performed poem.

At almost the last minute before the performance started Abigail arrived. Her two sticks soon cleared passage for her from the aisle to the seat between Becky and Grampa Graham.

"Sorry I'm late, Becky, but I don't move as fast as I used to. The thought of clambering off and on a tramcar was too much. I got a taxi. We're in for a treat. I wouldn't have missed this for anything."

The words were scarcely out of her mouth before a rallentando on the piano by a self-important, ramrod-stiff-backed woman announced the evening was about to commence.

Grampa Graham turned to Abigail to whom he'd just been introduced. "This should be grand. There's nothing like a good session of Rabbie Burns's poetry especially in January."

Abigail frowned. "Oh! But I rather think …"

Her words were drowned in a crashing of chords from the over-enthusiastic pianist at the side of the stage which startled the audience into attention. A large, overdressed lady came to the centre of the stage and announced in ringing tones: "Welcome, one and all. We'll start straight away with the junior poetry reading. All thirty boys and girls will recite the test piece – a gem of literature titled: *Cluck, cluck Aih'm a duck.*"

Becky could not resist stealing a glance at her father-in-law. His face bore a mixture of amazement, disappointment, and resentment. By the time the test piece had been recited twenty times with another ten still to go it was obvious that Grampa

Graham was not alone in his displeasure. From the captive audience came the sounds of much shuffling of bottoms on hard wooden seats; much rustling of sweetie pokes, caramel and chewing gum wrappers; and the scuffling of shoes and booted feet on the wooden floor.

When Val had finished her piece and, as far as Grampa Graham was concerned, covered herself with glory, he obviously considered the evening over. However a warning look from Becky and his wife's hawser-like grip kept him chained to his seat. When the last contestant had finally stumbled his weary way through, Cluck, Cluck, Aih'm a Duck, the comment rhyming with Duck from the man in seat in front of them, drew a reprimand of: "Language, please, there are ladies present," from Gramy Graham and a quickly hidden smile from Grampa.

# Chapter 22

After the poetry speaking competition, Val puffed up with pride at her success in her first bout of public speaking, insisted on taking her tin medal to school to show off to her teacher. It was doubtful if ever before any pupil at Greenfield School had enjoyed such a distinction and with the ever present emphasis on 'proper speaking' Val became something of a teacher's pet. She was even paraded round the other classes to demonstrate the shining example of speaking the 'King's English' as opposed to the guttersnipe language of the Glasgow dialect and the native Scots tongue.

Val so enjoyed her celebrity status that daily her speech patterns became more and more exaggerated and stilted. Soon her tortured vowels and prissy manners made her the butt of her immediate schoolmates and some of the older boys and girls in the Qualifying Class took to chasing her home and shouting obscenities at her. Gradually the bullying made Val miserable and Becky began to wonder if in her quest for perfection she had unleashed a monster into her daughter's life. Before she could reach a decision on what to do for the best, Grampa Graham, seeing his beloved Val cast in the role of a victim, stepped in.

"Becky, I know you set great store by all this elocution nonsense, but Val's got her medal to prove she's the best. Can you not just leave it at that?"

Although Becky was annoyed at Grampa Graham's interference she knew that in his direct, blunt approach he had echoed precisely her own thoughts on the matter. Even so, she felt herself to be on the horns of a dilemma. She suspected that Miss Andrews had come to depend on the weekly tuition fee and would therefore be loath to part with Val. The medal winner herself by this time was in no doubt – she agreed with Grampa.

Becky chewed at her lower lip as she thought: *The only loser in this will be Miss Andrews – fine recompense for the sterling efforts in producing a champion poetry speaker. I suppose a letter would do ... but, no, that's the coward's way out ... yes, I'll just have to go and tell her in person.*

It was with a feeling of impending doom that Becky finally made her way over to Bridgeton for the dreaded meeting. To make matters even harder, Miss Andrews gave Becky the same rapturous welcome as on her first visit to broach the subject of Val's lessons. As they sat over their teacups, Becky felt she was almost choking over the cream sponge as she put off the moment of truth. Placing her cup down and clearing her throat preparatory to launching into her much-rehearsed speech Becky took a closer look at her old friend and mentor.

*There's something different about her today,* Becky thought. *Oh, yes! Her hair! She's just had a Marcel Wave and doesn't she look smart without that awful stretched cardigan and work pinny – it looks like her teaching triumph in producing a winner has gone to her head. Oh, God, how in heaven's name can I now tell her of Val's decision to quit?*

However, before Becky could start her speech, Miss Andrews, after rather self-consciously patting her exaggerated hair style, leant forward and said: "Becky, there's something I have to tell you and I do hope it won't come as too much of a shock. But rules are rules and must be followed."

Becky, completely at a loss to understand what Miss Andrews was talking about, mumbled: "Rules? What rules are those, Miss Andrews?"

"It means that since I've been appointed an official adjudicator for many, if not all, public speaking events in the Glasgow area,

I'll no longer be able to teach or have any pupils of my own."

As the facts finally dawned on Becky she felt as though a great weight had been lifted form her back. She reached over to clasp Miss Andrews' hand. "Congratulations, Miss Andrews. What an honour – an adjudicator no less. I am really delighted for you. Please, please don't worry for a moment about Val …"

A slight frown creased Miss Andrews' brow. "Oh, but I do worry. You see it's all due to Val and her triumph in winning her medal and also to my other prize-winning students in higher grades that the powers-that-be have elected me to the Board of Adjudicators."

They sat for a while longer chatting then as Becky was leaving Miss Andrews said: "Thank you for being so understanding. You have no idea how anxious I was about telling you."

On her way back to Govan on the tramcar Becky thought: *Amazing! Half the things we worry about – agonise over – never actually happen. So let this be a lesson to you Becky Graham.*

# Chapter 23

Next day Val told her mother that Gramy and Grampa Graham had come up with a much better scheme to replace the now despised elocution. A project that she was sure would make her the envy of all the rampaging bullies from the 'Qually Class'. She would take dancing lessons.

On the Saturday evening after high tea Grampa Graham started outlining their grand plan for dancing lessons.

Ewan scowled. "What's all this? It's the first I've heard of it."

Grampa Graham smiled. "We've already talked it over with Val. She's all for it."

Gramy Graham nodded. "Yes, the wee pet, she can hardly wait to start on her dancing lessons. All excited she is."

Perhaps it was the fact that everything seemed to have been decided behind his back – the realisation that it was cut and dried without any reference to him as head of the house that annoyed him. Whatever the reason, Ewan, now red-faced with anger, was more upset than Becky had ever seen him before.

As she wondered how best to deal with the situation, Ewan demanded: "Just where, might I ask, is the money for this flight of fancy coming from? For the expense won't stop at the weekly fee for the lessons. Oh, no! There will be the expense of kitting her out in a dozen different costumes – Little Dutch Girl, Irish Colleen, not to mention the full Highland Regalia and the expense of dance competitions. All a complete and utter, bloody waste of my hard earned money, if you ask me."

His parents exchanged a glance, then his mother said: "Just hold your horses a minute, son. You've got the wrong end of the stick. It won't cost you a penny – we'll foot the bill."

"You? God in heaven, mother. Are you daft? I know fine that father's got a steady job – but times are hard. Men still get tossed on the unemployment scrap heap without even a minute's notice. I'll not allow you to waste your money like this."

Gramy Graham laughed. "Far from being sacked, your father's moved a step up. He's the day supervisor at the destructor with the night supervisor under him. It doesn't make a big difference in his pay, but after all these years it's enough we can afford to pay for Val's lessons."

In the end, as Ewan was always slightly in awe of his parents, Gramy and Grampa Graham won the day.

Every Friday night after school Becky and Val trotted along to a rented Govan church hall for Val's hour of instruction.

Ewan had, of course, been correct. It soon became apparent that not just one dance outfit would be needed in time, but instead a whole wardrobe of them. In discussing this with other mothers sitting on the chairs ranged round the walls of the practice room Becky soon became all too aware of the costs which could be incurred. She had been saving, in the tea caddy, the weekly amount that was no longer being spent on elocution lessons but that was going to be only a drop in the bucket.

Becky frowned as she thought of the expenses. Her new friend, Hannah Harper, whose own daughter was a gifted little dancer and was already the proud possessor of the correct outfits for every style of dancing, leaned forward and said: "Becky, there's no need to get yourself in a state about paying for costumes."

"And just how do you make that out, Hannah?"

"Use your head."

"Hmph! It'll take a bit more than that, I'm afraid."

Hannah laughed. "All you have to do is wait, watch, ask around – you'll soon see who is growing out of their outfits, then get in there quick and make a cash offer."

When Becky called at Crossloan Road to pick up Scott she mentioned this conversation to Gramy Graham.

She smiled and said: "I think Grampa already has the word out for his men to watch for any Highland stuff being ditched in the West End. Ewan always says it's amazing what toffs throw away."

# Chapter 24

It was fast as approaching the date of the annual dance exhibition to be held in South Govan Town Hall. Thanks to the progress made by young Val, her teacher decided that Val was proficient enough to take part in two items on the programme.

For the first part, that of a woodland nymph, Miss Fraser already had a stock of these hand-made, hand-me-down garments. These creations she dragged out from their moth-balled hideaway year after year for the now traditional finale. It was then the simple expedient of each child either squeezing into an over-tight dress or being tucked and pinned with a battery of safety pins into one which was sizes to large. None of Miss Fraser's woodland nymphs would ever have been allowed on stage in any other attire but these outfits constructed from sparkly green curtain material. Only one dancer in the troupe – the Fairy Queen herself – had a custom made costume. The champion dancer this year, with the much sought-after honour of being The Fairy Queen, was Val's bête-noire, Sadie.

For Val's other part a proper Highland outfit was a necessity and this Grampa Graham had provided. Becky's first sight of the eye-dazzling, garish tartan had startled her, but she kept this opinion to herself as Val was over the moon with delight.

As the curtain finally rose, albeit after a series of false starts, the long awaited dance exhibition finally got under way. As if to make up for lost time a rapid succession of tap-dancers, clog-dancers, and Irish colleens who shook their fists in the regulation

Irish washerwoman fashion appeared, but no sign of a Highland dancer.

Scott, by now wriggling in his seat, asked again, loudly: "Where's Val? I don't see Val, Mammy. Where is she?"

As she had been doing since the start of Scott's stream of questions, Gramy Graham fed him yet another chunk of coconut tablet from her rapidly diminishing supply. This saw him through a noisy routine of little drummer girls who, with a measure of expertise, tap-danced and banged on their toy drums, to end by saluting smartly to the audience before marching off-stage in rather ragged lines. As the ear-splitting noise of the drums and the clamour of applause died away Scott entertained himself by chasing down captive bits of coconut from between his teeth. Then, just as he opened his mouth for the inevitable question, a lone, aged and decrepit piper marched on stage to the skirl of his own version of a Highland marching tune. In his wake at last came the Highland dancers. Although not in the forefront it was impossible to miss the apparition that was Scott's sister, Val. The other dancers seemed to be wearing somewhat muted tartans, but Val in her red and yellow, 'Dress Macmillan' kilt and red velvet jacket stood out like a lighthouse beacon on a foggy night.

With a shout of joyous recognition Scott yelled: "There she is! Val! Yoo-hoo."

When it was announced with a roll of drums, the second half of the seemingly endless programme turned out to be a rerun of the first half. This time although the acts and set pieces were identical to those through which the audience had already suffered the difference was that this time they were performed by an older group of pupils. Although they were more confident and polished, they lacked the endearing charm, the two-left-footedness, of the baby class. Even so, since it was obvious the idea was to ensure that every single pupil of Miss Fraser had her own three minutes of fame most people took the view that what could not be cured must be endured.

When the stage-two troupe of Highland dancers appeared

minus the rainbow-hued Val, Scott set up such a hullabaloo in search of her that a grey-haired lady in front turned to face him. Instead of the rebuke, which Becky felt he richly deserved, the woman presented him with an entire paper-poke of long-chewing, teeth-destroying, dentist's friends toffee balls.

A final roll of drums from the tap-dancers announced that mercifully the end was approaching and the curtain fell. After several attempts to raise the curtain for the finale it finally rose only to crash halfway down to the platform, there to remain. The scene before the now restive audience was an enchanted forest onto which galumphed the star-spangled, wand-carrying Fairy Queen. Various other nymphs and shepherds wandered their weary self-conscious way through the magic forest and a would-be mischievous band of elfin helpers did unnecessary things around the stage.

Throughout this pantomime Scott grew increasingly fidgety looking for Val. Obviously the stupid Fairy Queen peering fruitlessly behind one cardboard tree after another couldn't find Val either. Like an eel, Scott slid from his seat, squirmed past the row of knees and sped down the centre aisle towards the brightly-lit stage to help in the search. Once up the stairs at the side of the platform, blinking in the glare of the footlights Scott's sturdy little figure became the centre of attention. There were gales of delighted laughter from the formerly semi-comatose audience as an irate Fairy Queen, whose artistic thunder had just been stolen, tried to shoo him off the stage and out of the enchanted forest. Scott body-swerved, avoiding the ever-more frantic swipes from the shiny, beribboned, magical, fairy wand, as he cavorted shouting: "Val, I can see you. This is great fun. Come out from behind that bush. It's your turn to chase me."

The victorious grande-finale descended into utter chaos as the recalcitrant curtain dramatically shot skywards from its previously stuck half-down position bearing with it a shrieking Fairy Queen whose wings had become entangled in the long silken fringes of the curtain.

# Chapter 25

That evening, after the fiasco of the dance exhibition Gramy Graham invited Ewan, Becky and the children round to Crossloan Road for a special high tea to celebrate the event.

Grampa Graham with tears of laughter in his eyes after the concert had said: "Ewan, lad, I hope you don't mean to chastise wee Scott for tonight. Man, it was grand. The best laugh I've had in years. Scott wasn't really being naughty – he was just being a normal wee lad. After all, it was hardly his fault that without the benefit of a single dance lesson he turned out to be the star of the show."

Gramy Graham had obviously pulled out all stops in her baking for the high tea and Becky watched with some alarm as the children stuffed themselves with millionaire's shortbread, jelly and mandarin oranges, and cherry-topped, iced Empire biscuits, but felt that in Gramy Graham's home she couldn't interfere.

When the dishes had been cleared away and the adults seated in the parlour Ewan turned to Grampa Graham. "Right, father, what about a tune for us? It's been a while since we heard the wee squeeze box."

After the expected ritual persuasion of a reluctant Grampa Graham, he did play for them then insisted that everyone else now had to do his or her turn. Even the normally reticent neighbour Mrs O'Conner, who had joined the tea party, was cajoled into doing her artistic best for the Emerald Isle. All turned now to Ewan.

"Right," he said rising to his feet. "To finish off our wee

ceilidh, I'll recite for you a little gem of literature called – wait for it – Cluck, cluck, Aih'm a duck."

Howls of protest and gales of laughter greeted this suggestion and the evening ended on this note.

Just as Becky was about to leave, Gramy Graham pulled her back and uncharacteristically enveloped Becky in a bear hug. Then holding her daughter-in-law at arm's length she said: "I've never said this to you before, but for some reason I feel I must say it now. I'm really glad you married Ewan. A wife like you was exactly what he needed. Becky, you're a grand lass, even though you can be a wee bit hard on the children."

Becky, on the point of tears, quickly kissed Gramy Graham on the cheek and hurried out after her family.

Next morning as Becky was busy preparing the children for Sunday School a frantic rapping on the door made her look in alarm at her husband. He at once put down his Brylcreem and moved to open the door. On the doorstep was Mrs O'Conner, not the carefully dressed party-goer of the previous evening, but a dishevelled, distraught looking woman.

"Can you come quick, son?" she blurted out. "It's your Mammy. She's been taken bad, really bad."

# Chapter 26

It was fast approaching Hogmanay, that last evening of the year for which every Scottish housewife worthy of the title scrubbed, dusted and polished everything in sight that did not actually move. Becky dived around her single end in a frenzy of cleaning, cooking and baking and found more and more that the children were getting under her feet. Finally, when she could stand their antics not a moment longer they had to go out. She realised it was far too cold to send them out to play either in the dank close or in the filthy back yard, but …

She lifted down the china teapot in which she stored her carefully garnered horde of silver threepennies and after counting out enough turned to Val. "You were a good wee girl helping Mammy earlier. So how would you like to take Scott to the pictures? There's a lovely show on at the Vogue. Scott will love seeing all the wee dwarfs and you, you'll like Snow White."

Val's joyous face was answer enough. No sooner were the children all happed up in their coats, hats and long woollen scarves than Becky felt a frisson of fear.

*Oh!* she thought, *this is exactly what those over-worked, harassed Paisley mothers did that tragic Hogmanay back in 1929. They sent their children off to a picture-house matinee just so they could get on with their house-cleaning for the New Year. No! Things have changed since the Paisley Glen Cinema fire. The Vogue's a new modern building and anyway surely such a coincidence is unthinkable.*

Never-the-less, Becky could not resist one last admonition. "Remember now, Val, you're the big one of the family. You're in charge of your wee brother. Just see that you take really good care of him. Do you understand?"

Val, by now hopping from foot to foot in an agony of suspense to be out of the flat and on their way, gave a hasty nod, and unceremoniously grabbing hold of her young brother headed towards the door and an afternoon of freedom in the comforting dark of the picture-house.

Her mother with a hand on her arm stopped her. "One last thing … you do not buy Scott pink bubble gum or gobstoppers with your spending money … oh, and no sweetie cigarettes either. I don't want him stuffing himself too full and being sick. Is that clear?"

In her very evident impatience to escape Val would have agreed to any condition her mother cared to inflict. She gave another quick nod and tightened her grip on Scott, but her mother wasn't finished. "One last thing …"

Val sighed.

"It's the Vogue you're to take him to and *not* that flea-pit of a place you went to last time. Apart from anything else it's a horror picture there and that would give Scott nightmares. So, off you go now … the Vogue, no rubbishy sweets, and no bubble gum … have a good time."

# Chapter 27

So engrossed was Becky with her many housewifely tasks she was scarcely aware of the short winter's afternoon speeding by. From the moment the children had left on their picture-going expedition Becky had worked tirelessly without so much as stopping for a cup of tea. Now she had one final task to undertake and after that she promised herself she would sit at the fireside for a break with a reviving cup of tea and a buttered scone. A quick glance at the clock was enough to reassure her she had time in hand before the children would re-appear, full of excitement about the picture they had seen and, of course, clamouring: "What's for tea, Mammy?"

Becky hauled a chair across the room to position it under the wooden shelf that ran the length of one wall. She clambered up onto the chair and started carefully lifting down the never-once-used collection of her precious wedding gift from Aunt Meg and Uncle Jack of Willow Pattern dinner plates. With the stack of plates successfully deposited on the kitchen table she gave a sigh of relief. Now for the massive, heavy soup tureen … big enough to feed an army on the march.

With a smile at the ridiculous mental image this thought created, Becky geared herself for the physical task of moving the huge dish safely down to the spot on the kitchen table already cleared for it. Balanced somewhat precariously on the creaking wooden chair and with her precious cargo aloft in her upstretched arms she was about to lower it to waist level before attempting to dismount from the chair. At that point, all hell broke loose.

The outer door of the single end burst open, a blast of freezing air rushed in from the common close beyond and Scott's wailing voice piteously announced: "Mammy, I'm choking. And I didn't like the big monster."

As Becky struggled to balance herself the tureen slipped from her hands. In a blur of blue and white it flew past her to crash to the floor in smithereens.

For what felt like an age Becky looked down at the scene below as if not only from a great distance but as if she were a disinterested bystander. Then, she climbed down from the chair and picked her way carefully through the shards of broken china to her weeping children.

A quick appraising glance told her that while Val was also weepy looking, of the two it was Scott who was the more distressed.

Becky bent down to him. "What's wrong, son? And what's all this talk about a big monster? There's no monster here, that was just your silly old Mammy perched on a chair and throwing her best china around. Nothing for you to worry about."

Scott wiped his eyes then his runny nose on the sleeve of his trench coat. For once, Becky bit back the words of admonition which sprang to her lips. Even so, when Scott started to speak Becky spotted that Val gave him a sisterly but warning look. Immediately on the alert, Becky gave Scott another cuddle. "What's wrong, dear? Never mind, Val, you can tell me. Tell your Mammy what ever it is. But I do assure you there are no monsters here."

"No monsters here, Mammy, but big horrible monsters in the picture-house. A bad man killing folks in a wax-works and ..."

Scott paused to draw breath and Becky said: "But I don't understand, Scott. I was sure you would have loved Snow White. It wasn't monsters it was wee dwarfs ..."

Even as she spoke the light dawned. Becky turned to Val and the one word 'Val' was enough to open the floodgates of tears, tantrums and an outpouring of confessions – sins of omission and commission.

"Mammy, there was a big queue for Snow White so we went to the Elder instead. Scott likes playing with Plasticine making models … so I thought the big picture was about wax-works and he would like that …"

Becky frowned. "All very commendable, I'm sure, Val. Just one thing; what exactly was the title of that picture?"

Val toed patterns in the shards of china still on the floor before finally saying: "It was The Terror of the Waxworks …"

Becky nodded grimly. Scott, now sensing he was the innocent party in their escapade, blurted out: "I was so scared I choked on my gobstopper. Then hiding under my coat from the monster I chewed on a big button … it came loose … and I've swallowed it."

The doctor, annoyed at being called out, was anything but sympathetic.

"The message made it sound like something serious – something sharp. A button will likely dissolve and he'll not come to any harm. Porridge and soft bread puddings for a day or so and what doesn't dissolve will pass through. Hardly worth your shilling for calling me out. Good day."

# Chapter 28

For some time now there had been rumours of war and some now argued the inevitability of an outbreak. For Becky, involved as she was in bringing up her little family as best she could, making every halfpenny do the work of ten, war and all its implications seemed but a distant threat.

However, all that changed one day in March 1939 when Becky and Ewan received a letter from a Mr R. M. Alerdice, Chief Education Officer for Glasgow. The letter, headed, 'Evacuation of children from Glasgow in the event of a National Emergency', outlined the plans the authorities had made. Becky read through the letter several times and realised that she, in common with all other Glasgow parents, was asked to consider, and decide, whether or not their children should be included in the arrangements for the crowded areas of large cities. Such plans would mean the children would be relocated to 'safer places if war should break out'. The children would gather at the primary school nearest to their home and older and younger children of the same family would, 'as far as possible', be evacuated together. They would go to the chosen places in the care of their teachers 'who would remain with them'. If they were to be scattered all over the countryside, Becky wondered, how could a classroom teacher 'remain' with all of them? The final promise in the letter was, 'they – the children – would live in the country where they would be welcome'.

Following the receipt of the bombshell letter, Becky and other mothers spent many a playtime outside the school gates discussing it.

One mother said: "Uch, ye can dae whit ye like, Becky, but for me they can gae it any fancy word they like, but naebody ... and Ah mean naebody is gonnae tak ma weans away frae me and cart them aff tae strangers in the wilds o Scotland."

Becky laid a hand on Liza's arm. "But, Liza, surely you can see, if war comes, then it stands to reason the children would be safer well away from the city and all its factories, railways, and shipyards."

Liza would have none of it. "But bluidy naethin! If some high heid yin o a chief education officer thinks he can dictate tae me, he can jist damned well think again."

Throughout the rest of the spring and on into the summer, the rows and blazing arguments raged on.

Etta, who had a son in Val's class, sided with Becky that unpleasant as it would be to be parted from their children they would be safer out of the city.

One day after a particularly upsetting slanging match with Liza, Etta and two other young mothers, Becky gave a grim smile at the thought: *Who needs an official war with all this going on? Anyway, it might never happen.*

# Chapter 29

On the first of September, 1939 the official evacuation got under way. As Becky looked at Val and Scott, already they seemed like strangers from some alien planet rather than her own normal, beloved children. This morning they stood with a cardboard-boxed gas mask slung over one shoulder and over the other a bulging schoolbag. From the latter peeped out a variety of socks, spare underwear, and even the toes of canvas gym shoes, their well-cuffed school sannies. Like all the other children now lined up in the school playground each wore an enamel mug on a string which hung nonchalantly somewhere between the gasmask case and the schoolbag. The final indignity was the detailed, named luggage label which had been previously prepared and then tied securely round the neck of each child.

Becky looked round at the other mothers, already giving the appearance of being red-eyed and haggard. She saw that many who had previously voiced their fierce opposition to the Evacuation Scheme and all it stood for had obviously caved in at the last minute. Liza was not one of them. She had stuck to her guns and was accordingly keeping her brood of steps-and-stairs weans safe at home and well away from the tears and trauma already apparent in the playground of the designated school that morning.

Parents had been advised they should take farewell of their children then and there in the school line-up, but if they felt they must, they would not be prevented from marching with their offspring to the nearest railway station. Becky, choking back her tears, chose the latter alternative, although knowing as she did she was merely putting off the inevitable, dreaded moment of parting when she would have to wave goodbye with whatever last reserves of composure she could muster.

The word of command was given. The military style crocodile marched through the streets. The only sounds to be heard from the marchers was weeping, whispered words of comfort from distraught mothers, and the ring of tackety boots on the cobbles. Shopkeepers stood in silence in their shop doorways; even the normally raucous, bugle-playing fish-wife was subdued; a local postie stood cap in hand as though paying due and proper respect to a passing hearse.

When the line of children and their supporters finally turned into the railway marshalling area all hell broke loose. In a flash, at the sight of the waiting train, the reality of the coming departure, separation and loss could no longer be delayed. On all sides there were screams, loud weeping and frustrated tantrums from the children and from the mothers an emotional tidal wave of sobbing, keening, and hysteria.

Surveying this, the headmaster called out something unintelligible which Becky assumed was an instruction of some kind, but no one paid the slightest heed. Next, he blew a blast on his 'thunderer' whistle with equally little effect and it seemed that the situation was about to dissolve into utter chaos. Despite his bulk the school janitor heaved himself up onto a nearby wicker hamper. From this vantage point, he clanged the hand-held brass school bell he had had the foresight to bring along. As if miraculously, there was a dramatic and eerie silence. Throughout their schooldays the children had been conditioned to obey this hand-tolled summons immediately or suffer the dire consequences.

"Right, youse yins," the janitor shouted into the silence. "Just listen weel tae yer heidmaister. He's in charge."

He jumped down and before the headmaster knew what was happening he was being given a leg-up to the vacated perch. Now he was able to order the children on their way, out of the arms of weeping mothers and off on the first stage of their journey to ‘a chosen place where they would live in the country, in houses where they would be made welcome’.

As Becky looked at her two weeping children she prayed earnestly that all the blithe, official promises would be kept and that her bairns would indeed be welcome … and above all well-cared for.

At the final moment of parting Becky gave them a last, lingering hug and whispered to Val: “Remember now, be a good girl and make sure you take good care of your wee brother. Promise now?”

After watching the train steam out of the station Becky turned away and started the trudge home … to an empty house.

# Chapter 30

For Becky the weeks in the aftermath of the piteous farewells and the departure of her children seemed endless and empty. Apart from the time when Scott had been at death's door in the Fever Hospital with diphtheria, she had never, before or since, been separated from either of her children. Now her single end, empty and deathly quiet without the vitally alive presence of Val and Scott, seemed desolate and hardly even a home. To make matters worse, Ewan's way of coping with the unnatural situation was to keep working even longer hours which meant that when he did come home he was tired and irritable and in no mood to listen to a catalogue of Becky's moans and real or imaginary problems.

For want of something else to occupy her hands and mind, Becky swept, dusted and polished her wee palace until not an inch of untreated floor, fabric, or furniture remained. The one bright spot in the week was when postie would drop a postcard through the letterbox. Even that, after the initial joy of getting it, would soon prove to be an even greater source of worry. Val's carefully written, almost over-correct message invariably gave the impression of having been dictated by her teacher. The terse, stilted sentences gave away nothing of any worth to indicate what was actually happening.

Becky peered at the latest postcard with its non-committal: "I am fine, Mammy. Scott is fine, a good boy at school. I hope you and Daddy are fine too." She frowned and held the card up to the light coming through the kitchen window to scrutinise it even better.

*Well, there's a thing*, she thought. *Either this card's been left out in the rain, or postie has dropped it in a puddle, or my poor wee Val's been weeping over it.*

She was deep in thought when she heard a knock on the door.

"Oh, it's yourself, Etta. You're early on the go today. But it's always a pleasure to see you. Come away in and I'll get us a cup of tea."

Becky ushered her friend into her home and got her comfortably seated beside the fire. It was obvious to the most casual glance that Etta had been weeping and Becky bustled around at the stove waiting patiently for Etta to tell her what the problem was.

When Etta did start to talk it was such a jumble of ill-assorted ideas poured out in a torrent of tears that Becky stopped her. "Listen, Etta, suppose we take this a bit slower. To let me get the facts right, can I ask you questions on what I think I've gathered so far?"

Etta nodded.

"Right, today you had a postcard from your Alan? Sounds the same as mine. Just the usual standard stilted message – I am well, hope you are too, I am happy here on Arran, school is good – have I got it right?"

Etta blew her nose vigorously then with a snort of disgust said: "That's it exactly, Becky, exactly, damn near word for word. No worth a tuppenny dam those postcards … they just say the same bluidy rubbish week after week. They tell us naethin. An insult tae oor intelligence so they are."

Becky nodded. "But that's old news, isn't it? We've talked about these cards before. You said something about another letter you had by the same post this morning. I couldn't quite catch what you were saying about that."

Etta sat up straighter in her chair. "It's like this, Becky. John … a cousin of mine … he works on the Clyde ferries. Usually he does the Rothesay run, but wee while back he was shifted tae the Arran boat. So, when he was on the island anyway, on his day off, he thought he'd take the chance tae find oot how my bairns were really gettin on in their evacuation billets."

When Etta paused, Becky urged: "Go on, Etta tell me."

"Ye're no gonnae like this, but Ah felt it ma Christian duty tae share this wi ye. Ah don't mind tellin ye it ferr broke ma hert when Ah read yon letter frae John."

Becky felt like strangling Etta who now seemed to be enjoying the drama of her recitation.

"Remember what that bastard Education Officer telt us? Aw that guff aboot the evacuees bein made welcome? Well, devil the fear o that!

"John says when he talked tae folks aboot the evacuees in the pub he was telt there were some 'private' evacuees that had been brought over by their mothers and settled with islanders that wanted tae take them in – for so much a week … like in a boardin hoose on the holidays. The other evacuees – the Glesca keelies – that came ower by the barrowload in September were dumped on whoever had empty rooms without as much as a by-your-leave. Some o them, he was telt, are fine and got good places but others could be haein a real rough time."

"Did John do anything else – except I mean sit in the pub and talk?"

"Oh, aye, the next time he was on the island for a day he managed tae get a lift oot o Broderick up the coast a bit tae a wee village. It turns oot that yer twa are in the same village as my Alan and Teena. He didnae get tae speak tae yer weans, but he managed tae speak tae Alan. He's aw right, but he and Teena dinnae like the food – although he says there's plenty o it. John says maist o the teachers frae Greenfield didn't stay on the island and the ones that did are all in the town and only come out tae see the weans in the villages aff and on. And Alan says the village kids make fun of him and Teena and he's had a couple of fights."

"Etta, can you scrape up enough for train and ferry fares to Arran?"

"Aye, Ah think so."

"Good, we're going to Arran to see for ourselves."

# Chapter 31

Becky and Etta descended on Arran in early December, 1939, knowing only the village where the children were billeted and Becky decided to go straight to the school. They arrived just as the afternoon session was about to start and when Val and Scott saw Becky at the school gate they ran to her.

"Mammy!" Scott shouted. "Can we go home?"

Becky hugged both of them and took a good look. Neither seemed any the worse off from their stay. Scott if anything seemed to have put a little weight on his skinny frame.

"Are you both all right?" Becky asked.

Both burst into tears.

"I don't like it here," Scott said. "I want to go home."

Val snuffled her agreement.

"What's wrong? Is anybody being bad to you?"

"No," Val said, "Mr and Mrs Carter are okay, but it's not home. Please can we come home?"

"They made us eat a rabbit," Scott said. "I was sick."

Before Becky could answer them the teacher of the one-roomed school appeared to find out what all the commotion was in the yard.

"Who are you?" she demanded of Becky and Etta.

When Becky introduced herself and Etta the teacher frowned.

"You shouldn't be here. You'll just upset the children. They were only beginning to settle down. Homesickness is quite natural first time away from home. They'll get over it soon and be right as rain."

"No," Becky said, "they're going home with us."

The four children cheered.

"I can't possibly allow that," the teacher said. "This is most irregular. There must be forms to fill out. You'll need to talk to the authorities and come back when everything is in order. Unless you do that you are breaking the law – kidnapping."

"Rubbish!" Becky said. "They're my children. You can't kidnap your own children. So my two are going with me. What about you, Etta?"

Etta swallowed. "Weel, Ah dinae want tae get intae trouble with the authorities, but if ye think it's okay, Becky, Ah'm wi ye."

"Right, Val and Scott, is there anything you need to get from the school?"

Both shook their heads.

"Right, we'll go and pick up your stuff from … Mrs Carter, wasn't it? Etta, get your two to take you to where they've been living and meet us at the bus stop. The driver said there'd be a bus back in time for the ferry."

The teacher frowned. "I can't physically stop you–"

"Naw and ye'd better no try," Etta said.

"But I will inform the police."

Alan, Etta's son, laughed. "The school disnae hae a phone and the nearest polis is twa miles away roon the coast. By the time he finds oot and gets here on his bike we should be hame."

Triumphantly, Becky marched her two to the cottage where they'd been billeted. Mrs Carter, a stout country woman, shrugged when Becky announced her intention of taking Val and Scott back to Glasgow.

"They've both been pining for home, particularly Scott. They've been good, biddable children – not like some of the Glasgow keelies other folks have had to put up with. What did Miss Owens say?"

"Who? Oh, the school-teacher?" Becky relayed the conversation and Mrs Carter laughed.

"Oh, yes, she's a stickler for forms – *i*'s dotted *t*'s crossed and all that sort of thing." Mrs Carter glanced at the clock on the mantle-piece. "You'll have time for a cup of tea and a scone before the bus while the children collect their bits and pieces – not that they brought much with them."

Becky started to apologise for the sparse wardrobe the children had arrived with but Mrs Carter waved her excuses aside.

"I know, they were just allowed what they could carry in their school bags. The Woman's Rural had stuff they'd collected for the evacuees, but I had some clothes I should have thrown out years ago when my children grew out of them so I had plenty for your two."

Back on the mainland and safely aboard a train bound for Glasgow Central Station Becky and Etta had time to sit back and congratulate themselves on the successful completion of their daring rescue.

Etta wept copiously at the state of her children's heads. Alan's formerly wavy hair had been shaved off, leaving only an upstanding tuft – a scalping lock – like an obscene insult above his forehead. Teena, bereft of her golden curls, now sported a pudding-basin cut complete with a short fringe which certainly wasn't worth the title of a can-can.

"Those women – the Women's Rural or whatever they call themselves – they were the ones that met the weans aff the boat and herded them intae a church hall tae parcel them oot. They decided that ony weans frae Glesca just *had* tae be lousy, so the easiest thing tae dae was to shave their heads. Tae think o the time – tae say naethin o the money – Ah spent ivery Friday night wi the bone comb and the Derback Soap makin sure Alan and Teeny hadnae picked up ony livestock. Those women wouldnae even take the time to check for nits – och naw, just shave the lot!"

Becky looked in wonder at Val's fat bouncy ringlets and Scott's still luxuriant, undamaged waves.

"Then how?" she started.

Alan laughed. "When Val saw what was happenin, she said something tae Scott. Next thing he was on the floor haein a real paddy – it was rerr, screamin and shoutin, bangin his feet on the floor, the works. Ye could a heard him clear across the Clyde. One o the women said something tae the others and picked Scott up and took him and Val away. Next time Ah saw them was at the village and their hair hadnae been cut."

"It was Mrs Carter," Val said. "She said she'd take us. The other women laughed and said: 'On your head be it,' whatever that meant. She went over our hair just the way you do, Mammy."

The school bell was clanging to call the children back into the building for the remainder of the morning's lessons and mothers were already turning away from the gates as Becky neared the top of Elderpark Street.

Catching sight of her friend, Becky waved frantically and called out in a fashion totally unlike her normal more ladylike behaviour. Hearing her name shouted like this, Etta left the knot of women she was with and made her way across to join Becky. By now breathless from her exertions and from the sheer excitement of her news, it was a moment before Becky could compose herself sufficiently to say: "Etta, it's come! That letter … the official letter and …"

But before Becky could say another word, she saw that Etta had gone deathly pale.

"Oh, my God, Becky! Whit will they dae tae us? Put us in gaol? Uch, Ah ken fine we were desperate tae get oor weans hame – but we should never hae taen the law intae oor ain hauns. Oh, see ma man – he'll gae berserk when he hears this. He'll gae me a right beltin, even though it's no a Friday or Saturday."

Becky put a hand on Etta's arm to try to stop the flood of words and finally almost shouted: "Etta! For heaven's sake stop talking and listen. All right – I said I had an official letter, but it's not from the Chief Education Officer – it's from Glasgow City council and–"

At these words Etta seemed on the point of collapse. "God help us! The council. That's even worse."

Becky laughed. "Worse? No, no it couldn't be better. It's nothing to do with our high jinks in Arran. This official letter – it's to advise me that I've been allocated a council house. A council house, no less! Now, what do you think of that?"

Etta stared as if such news was almost too much to comprehend. Finally, she grinned. "Ah think yer wan lucky deil – if ye fell intae the Clyde ye'd come up wi a gold watch. Ah'll tell ye somethin else. Wance yer in yer new cooncil hoose ye'll be that toffee nosed and posh ye'll no be wantin tae associate wi a known kidnapper like me."

# Chapter 32

The council house in nearby Drumoyne was all, and more, than anything Becky had dreamed of. Four-in-a-block with two houses upstairs and two down. Ewan and Becky had one of the upstairs houses. A good sized living room with a smart fireplace for the coal fire, a spanking new kitchen complete with good deep sinks and a clothes boiler, two bedrooms, and, joy of joys, a bathroom.

If Becky was in her seventh heaven, it was nothing to Ewan's pride of ownership in his very own strip of garden to the side and the back of the four-in-a-block building. There was even a shared patch of lawn, complete with clothes poles, and a strict rota setting out whose turn it was to hang out washing.

*Yes,* Becky thought, *one way and another everything in the garden is lovely.*

However, one night as the family slept uneasily in the Anderson Shelter in the back garden, the sound of bombs, crashing masonry and shattering glass grew even closer. When the all clear sounded and they all trooped upstairs to their home Becky took one look at the smashed windows and burst into tears.

Ewan did his best to comfort his wife and children but pointed out: "We're lucky, Becky. Broken glass we can sweep up. Windows can be fixed. We still have our house. There must be folks right now looking at ruins that used to be their homes. But this settles it – the war has started in earnest now. We'll have to see about getting the children away back to the safety of the country."

Becky looked in horror at her husband.

"Yes," he went on, "evacuation. It seems the authorities were right after all. The children would be much safer out of the city."

Becky agreed but for this evacuation she would have no dealings with officialdom.

Instead, through the services of a friend who had a relative in the country, it was arranged the children would be re-evacuated privately to the safety of a pig farm in Lanarkshire. However, given the horrendous treatment meted out to the Govan evacuees on Arran when the children had had their heads shaved to delouse them before being sent to homes 'where they would be made welcome', even the prospect of the more socially elevated private evacuation was not enough for Becky.

"No! They'll have to have someone of their own with them – a responsible adult who'll look out for them."

When Ewan had suggested that Becky should go with the children she had refused. Her place was at home looking after Ewan.

"Who then?" Ewan said. "Your mother's out of it. She's still in that old folk's place since her stroke last year. Your Aunt Meg would love to be with them, but I don't see her leaving Uncle Jack on his own, and Uncle Jack can't just waltz away from his bank. He's at least four years away from being able to retire."

"Well, I wouldn't trust Erchie on his own with them even when he is sober. What about your father, Ewan?"

"Oh, for heaven's sake, Becky. You know what he's been like ever since my mother died. Between that and being retired in the spring, he just creeps around like a lost soul. Nothing to do and all day to do it."

"Right, Ewan. He's ideal. He's retired. There's nothing to keep him in town. It'll give him a new purpose in life, a bit of responsibility again. Something else – someone else – to think about beside his own misery."

A week later Val, Scott, and Grampa Graham set out on their adventure. This time there were no frantic scenes in the school playground, no screams at the railway station, and no attempted shearing of young heads and therefore no need for Val to incite Scott to stage his tantrum which had saved their hair in Arran.

Grampa Graham, already with a new spring in his step, was fully in charge and determined that this time everything would go well for his beloved grandchildren.

# Chapter 33

This time instead of the ultra-correct, say-nothing postcards from Arran there were newsy letters full of their doings, their new school, and their joy at living the freedom of an unfettered life in the country. Becky read Val's most recent letter for about the tenth time and smiled.

*Yes, it does seem to be going well,* she thought. *From what Val says it sounds as if Grampa Graham has found a new lease of life. Just wait till I tell Ewan this latest snippet.*

That evening when Ewan finally pushed away his empty plate he said: "That was grand, Becky, just grand."

Becky laughed. "I see you've left the pattern on the plate at least. There was another lovely letter from Val today. They're having a great time in the country."

Ewan nodded, then aware that Becky was expecting some comment from him said: "That's good. And what about Father? How's he been behaving himself?"

"Funny you should say that. Your dad's been great. He even sometimes walks the three miles into Biggar to take the bairns to the pictures. But there's something else ..."

"Nothing wrong with the old man is there?"

Becky laughed. "I don't know that he sees himself as an old man any more. In fact, if Val is to be believed, not only has he discovered the fountain of youth, your father has found himself a girlfriend."

Ewan's eyes widened in amazement, but before he could

comment Becky went on: "Mind you, I don't know that *girl*friend is an accurate description. She's a widow-woman, the mother of the lad that owns the pig farm. Seems she's a rich widow-woman and as Val puts it Mrs Meikle thinks Grampa Graham is the bees' knees."

# Chapter 34

After the Clydebank Blitz of March 13 and 14 and the Greenock Blitz of May 7 and 8, 1941 Becky and Ewan felt themselves very lucky to have escaped with nothing more daunting and life threatening than the shattered window panes experienced the previous November.

However, by early August the tone of Val's cheerful letters changed. There were now reports from Grampa Graham that he and the bairns – real townies all of them – were becoming more than a little disillusioned with the tram-car-free isolation and 'nothing much to do' aspect of country living. They were definitely not looking forward to the coming winter, especially if was to be a repeat of the last with horrendous snowdrifts and cold.

Becky had just finished reading the latest catalogue of moans to Ewan and he commented: "Sounds to me, whether we like it or not, as if they'll be arriving on our doorstep any day now."

"And reading between the lines it seems as if your father's grand romance with the pig-farmer's mother has hit a rocky patch, if not finished altogether."

Ewan laughed. "And just as well! Really, think on it. Can you imagine my father at his age getting all gooey-eyed over some old widow-woman? Daft old coot."

For a moment Becky said nothing, a little startled at the vehemence with which Ewan delivered his opinion of any possible romantic union between the two elderly people.

"Suppose I write today," Becky finally suggested, "and

suggest, if they really want to do so, that they could all come back to Glasgow. There's really not been all that much in the way of raids in Scotland since May. Sergeant Murray says he doesn't think there'll be any more big raids here."

In the event no second invitation was needed, and it seemed not even the courtesy of a written reply. The next week Becky answered a knock on the door to find the wanderers had returned.

Val, now twelve, had written the Lanarkshire 'Quallies' in June and Becky, armed with the result and Val's report, called on the headmaster of Govan High School – Mr Irvine. He looked carefully at the papers Becky gave him.

"Yes, Mother Graham, Val is certainly entitled to enter first year here in September … but a country school … hmm. I think it would be best if we placed her in the non-academic stream."

"She was only in the country school for six or seven months, the rest of her schooling was a Greenfield School and I know that has a good reputation."

"True … but still … she was evacuated at the outbreak of war wasn't she?"

"For a little over three months. Val is a bright girl. I know she'll do well."

Mr Irvine pursed his lips. "I'm reluctant to put a child with this background in the academic stream. In any case, she's a girl, and likely will be married before you know it."

"There's nothing wrong with her background." Becky bristled. "Why don't you let her into the academic stream for first year. If it proves too hard for her and she doesn't do well then I guarantee you can transfer her to the non-academic stream with no argument from me."

"Very well, Mother Graham, you can be quite persuasive."

So in September 1941 Val started at Govan High School.

Scott was re-established at Greenfield School and Grampa Graham was back in his flat in Crossloan Road.

Becky counted her blessings that in such a time of war she had her family safely round her. Even her fear that Ewan might be called up for the forces was in the past. At forty-two, when the war started, he certainly wasn't in the first age group to be called up. Now that the restaurant was officially classified as an auxiliary canteen for the shipyard workers and allotted rations accordingly, Ewan's work there meant that he was not eligible to be drafted into other 'War-related essential occupations'.

Since the evacuees' return from the country one thing puzzled Becky and it finally got to the point where she felt she had to discuss it with Ewan.

Having listened more or less patiently to Becky, Ewan said: "For heaven's sake, Becky. I can't think what all the fuss is about. If my father doesn't want to come to our 'special family teas' since he's come back from Lanarkshire, so what? It's not exactly earth shattering is it? At least it saves from having to listen to all his old stories again."

"Trust a man to feel that way. Say what you like Ewan but I think Grampa is hiding something. On the odd occasions we have seen him he hasn't once mentioned the widow-woman. Now he's taken to dotting back and forward to Partick every five minutes across the Govan Ferry. What exactly is that about?"

Ewan laughed. "Likely he's just trying to mend his broken heart with a dose of culture at the Kelvingrove Art Gallery, now that he's retired and the time is his own. Let's face it, the statues, pictures and ship's models at the gallery are bound to be more uplifting than what he looked at day in day out as the supervisor at the destructor."

There the matter had rested until the week before Scott's tenth birthday in November when Becky cornered Grampa Graham in his flat.

"We're having a wee special tea a week on Sunday. We'd like you to come, but if as usual these days ..." Becky's words trailed off.

"Becky, of course I'll come," Grampa said. "It's not every day my only grandson turns ten, is it? There's just one thing, Becky."

"Anything, Grampa. We'll be only too pleased to see you at the family tea table again. Is there something special you want?"

Looking embarrassed, Grampa Graham started fiddling with his pipe. When the cleaning and tamping in of new tobacco was completed to his satisfaction he looked up with a sheepish grin.

"No, it wasn't anything special to eat I had in mind. I was wondering … would it be all right with you if … if … Can I bring a friend with me to the birthday tea?"

In the days leading up to Scott's birthday Grampa Graham made no further reference to his 'bringing along a friend'. Becky had her own thoughts as to who the friend might be, but she thought it best to keep such preposterous ideas to herself. Time enough to warn Ewan of the extra guest on the big day itself.

However, Becky was so busy with her preparations and with keeping the children from fighting that everything else went out of her mind. When Ewan opened to door to admit his father he was startled to find a tweed-suited elderly woman by his father's side holding his arm in a proprietorial manner.

As the stern-looking Mrs Meikle was ushered into the living room, there was no shout of welcome from the children. Each raised eyes heavenwards at the very sight of this controlling relic from their exile in the Lanarkshire countryside. Not only had she arrived empty-handed, but as the meal progressed it was soon clear that, filthy rich or not, Mrs Meikle hated money being spent – even if it was not *her* money. With almost every mouthful of food, with every dainty sweet bite she lifted from the cake stand she intoned in a voice of doom: "Fair eating money, this is. Just fair eating money."

Despite this Greek chorus they got through the meal. Scott blew out his candles and Becky handed round the portions of home-made Victoria sponge. On the point of rising from the table Grampa Graham cleared his throat. "Now, I know this is Scott's big day, but since this is a family occasion this is as good a time as any to say … to let you all know …"

When it looked as if Grampa Graham was at a loss for words,

Mrs Meikle folded her arms across her ample bosom, fixed him with a steady gaze and said quietly: "Go on."

"Mistress Meikle – already known and loved by our birthday boy here and wee Val – Mistress Meikle has this day consented to be my wife."

A stunned silence greeted this announcement before Scott, the so-called fan of the bride-to-be, lifted an Empire biscuit to his lips and said: "Fair eating money, this is. Fair eating money."

# Chapter 35

No shot gun wedding for a besotted young couple was ever more quickly arranged than elderly Mrs Meikle's unseemly haste in getting Grampa Graham to the altar, or in their case to the Registry Office. In the lead-up to the nuptials it turned out that Grampa's recent frequent visits to Partick had been to visit his beloved. Doubtless in pursuit of her prey, she had chosen to lodge with a cousin in Dumbarton Road 'for a wee holiday'.

From all of this it seemed clear to Becky that once having set her cap at the old man, Mrs Meikle was not about to let him escape her clutches. While not entirely happy with the situation, Ewan and Becky could only make the best of it. When Ewan suggested as their wedding gift to the happy couple he would stand the cost of the celebration high tea followed by a visit to one of the city's cinemas the offer was promptly accepted.

On the big day following the ceremony the family party adjourned to the Ca'dora tea rooms for high tea. While Val and Scott were in their element at the sight of the small collection of French cakes to follow the main course, the bride, resplendent in her best, but somewhat battered, tweed suit and enormous jumble-sale hat, could only reiterate at frequent intervals: "Fair eating money! All this spread, it's just fair eating money."

Becky, wearying of this monotonous chorus turned to Ewan and whispered: "It's not even her money, for heaven's sake. We're the ones who should be moaning."

Ewan grinned and whispered back: "Never mind, Becky.

Money is like a god to her. By all accounts the old skinflint's loaded … not that my father's likely to see a brass farthing of it."

In the cinema throughout the performance Becky became aware that everyone who sat behind the still behatted bride would sit for a moment then, usually with a curse, shuffle off to another seat. When the lights came on in the hall for the interval, Becky glanced along the row intending to smile at her new mother-in-law and ask her if she would like a peppermint-cream. Instead she started to giggle and then collapsed into gales of helpless laughter. The bride, already tall and well built, was sitting head and shoulders above everyone else. Between that and the hat it was little wonder that no-one had wanted to sit behind her. Becky, muffling her laughter as best she could, nudged Ewan in the ribs and pointed to the source of her merriment.

Ewan too started to laugh. "Oh, good Lord. She can't ever have been in a cinema or a theatre before. She doesn't know … and no-one's had the gumption to tell her you're supposed to tip the seat down before you sit on it."

After a whispered conversation with Val she was dispatched along the row to advise the bride she would be much more comfortable if she cared to lower the seat rather than sit on the rim.

"Talk about a night to remember," Ewan said at home later. "I hope Dad's pleased with his new wife. Anyone more different from my mother would be hard to find. There'll be changes afoot for my father in the not too distant future – and I'll bet they'll not be for the better, you mark my words."

# Chapter 36

Early in 1942, the year following the wedding, Grampa Graham said to Becky: "We're thinking of moving out of the Crossloan Road flat."

Surprised, Becky said: "But you've lived there for years, Grampa. You love that wee room and kitchen."

Grampa Graham nodded but made no further comment. With a flash of inspiration the reason for the move struck Becky.

"Oh, hold on, I see. It's not good enough for your new wife! With her money she'll be wanting a real house and not just a tenement flat."

"Not exactly, Becky. You've got the wrong end of the stick. Elspeth feels the Crossloan Road flat is too big for just the two of us. The more room we have, the more there is to heat and light, the more visitors we'll be getting to stay from Lanarkshire. And all that will cost good money."

"But Grampa, apart from anything else the flat's so handy for Greenfield school. You know how Val and Scott love to pop in and –"

"Lassie, lassie, do you not see – she even grudges the expense of buying the wee sweetie biscuits for the bairns."

"I don't believe I'm hearing this. Well, Grampa, far be it from me to cause you any extra expense – it'll be the last time they drop in for a visit. I do assure you."

"Don't go into the huff with me, Becky. But you're right. It will be the last time they'll have such freedom to come and go.

We're moving come Quarter Day. Elspeth has found us a cheap single end to rent in Golspie Street."

"What! For heaven's sake, have you taken leave of your senses? Golspie Street! What in God's name are you thinking of?"

Grampa sighed. "It's not me. It's her. The move is definitely arranged; already she's unscrewed all the doorknobs inside the flat; she's bagged the last of the dross from the bottom of the coal bunker – she's made up her mind."

After the excitement of the wedding and the subsequent removal of the happy couple to Golspie Street, life once again settled into a routine for Becky, Ewan, and the children. The latter did miss the freedom of popping in to see Grampa every day after school, but there was something else to look forward to. They now had a regular weekly visit with him to the Elder Park and the luxury of some sweets bought on Grampa's sweetie ration coupons, although they missed the ice cream treats they used to get from Nottriano's Ice Cream Parlour on Govan Road, now closed and boarded up since the anti-Italian riots of June last year when Italy declared war on the side of Germany. Although no one ever actually voiced the thought, what added to their pleasure was the absence of Elspeth who kept to the seclusion of the single end rather than risk 'eating good money' in the form of any off-ration treats Grampa might buy.

One such early spring day with the children happily off on their weekly jaunt with Grampa, Becky, on a whim, decided to do a bit of spring cleaning. Not content to merely brush over the rugs where they lay in the living room, the hint of weak, long-awaited sunshine encouraged Becky to take the rugs out to the green in the back garden. There, after heaving them onto the clothes line, she started to beat them thoroughly with the long-handled, cane carpet beater. Even as she pounded away at them she thought: *Why don't I do this properly ... give them a good sponge down with that new cleaning liquid I bought from the Kleeneezee man at the door the other day?*

Suiting the action to the thought Becky ran upstairs to the kitchen. Although the metal cap came off easily enough, the cork had been rammed in so tightly it refused to budge. Finally, the corkscrew pulled the cork out but not before the neck of the bottle had been chipped. The raw edge nicked the skin of Becky's right hand between thumb and forefinger. Determined to press on with her cleaning operations, Becky dabbed at the blood with her apron then headed back out to the garden. Later, with the rugs hung over the washing line to dry, Becky felt a glow of satisfaction at a job well done.

When Becky started to clear the table after feeding Grampa and the children following their outing, the cut on her hand bled again.

"What's happened to your hand, Becky?" Grampa asked.

Becky dabbed at the tiny cut with the dishtowel. "It's nothing, Grampa. Just a wee nick in the skin."

"Well, make sure you keep it clean. Many a soldier in the trenches of the Great War got tetanus from such a cut and as I see, you've been out in the garden beating the dust, and the living daylights, out of your carpets."

Becky laughed.

# Chapter 37

Becky opened her eyes in a total panic.

Where was she? What had happened to her? Why was she wracked with pain?

Ewan's voice came from very far away, but she couldn't make out what he was saying.

Another voice seemingly closer this time said: "We've just given her another injection of a sedative to try to calm her down. The blood poisoning is very far advanced. We've done what we can to try to localise it but … We'll give it another couple of hours … but we may have to amputate the right arm at least as far as the elbow to stop the poison spreading and killing her."

"What about that stuff the other doctor mentioned?"

"Penicillin? That's what we're trying. It's certainly worked wonders with the war wounded since 1940. We'll have to wait and see how she responds. I'm sorry, but it's her last and only hope, even if we do amputate there's no guarantee …"

When Becky again surfaced she remembered the snatches of conversation about an arm being amputated. With what strength she could muster and filled with dread as to what she might find Becky struggled to withdraw her left arm from the confining bed sheets.

A cool hand caught hers and a kindly voice said: "Ah, so you're awake at last, Mrs Graham. You're lucky … the doctors did manage to save your arm. I'll be right back."

The nurse returned shortly with a doctor who pulled a chair over and sat at Becky's bedside.

"What you had, Mrs Graham, was tetanus – blood poisoning. You must have had a cut somewhere on your hand that became infected. We have managed to save your right arm ... but I'm afraid the hand is quite badly damaged and we had to remove the little finger."

Becky tried to struggle up to look at her right arm.

"Just lie still for now, my dear. There's nothing for you to see except bandages."

Slumping back, Becky said: "Why isn't Ewan here?"

"Your husband has been here every day for the last three weeks–"

"Three weeks? How ...?"

"You've been under sedation – morphine – to control the spasms. I don't expect you'll remember anything of those weeks. Just lie back and rest now."

Some time later Becky saw her arm. Yes, the brilliant surgeons had saved the arm but the legacy of the battle with tetanus was a cruelly disfigured right hand. Minus the pinkie, her hand was as solid and immovable as the carved hand of any marble statue in the Kelvingrove Art Gallery. The hand had been set, as the surgeon explained, with the fingers and thumb curved slightly inwards so that objects of a suitable size could be grasped. Jammed in, was how Becky thought of it.

When Becky was well enough to ask about how Ewan had coped while she was in hospital she was astounded to hear that the despised Elspeth had stepped into the breach. She had moved herself into Becky and Ewan's bedroom, leaving Grampa Graham in the single end, and relegating Ewan to sleep on the couch in the living room.

"Give her her due," Ewan said. "Skinflint and country bumpkin she may be but she does know how to run a house. She's kept everything just the way you do – polished to within an inch of its life. The bairns off to school, well turned out, and good healthy meals every day. I suggested I could bring some meals home from the restaurant and she went up like a blue light. She did finally say that my father, if he wished, instead of coming to our house, could perhaps have the odd meal there – 'I'm sure you won't charge your own father. I won't have him wasting good money when he could eat here with the bairns.'"

For the first time in six weeks Becky laughed.

Becky learned that while she had been *non-compus mentis* Nellie, her 'mammy' had died. Ewan commented to his father that Becky's lack of reaction to the news was probably because she was still to some extent under the influence of sedatives.

Homecoming, a week later, was a joyful affair. Becky was surprised that in that short time the children had both grown. Their delight in having Mammy back was obvious.

When Becky tried to thank Elspeth her attempt was brushed aside.

"I did no more than my Christian duty for my husband's grandchildren. There is no need to thank me. Thank the Lord for your deliverance. Now, I've left cottage pie in the oven for your tea tonight. Mr Graham and I will be off. Who knows what sort of mess he's got the single end into."

"Won't you stay and share tea with us? I'm sure there will be plenty to go round."

"No, I have a smaller dish of the pie in here," she held up her shopping bag. "There's enough pie for you and the bairns – Ewan can eat at the restaurant, I'm sure – what's not sold shouldn't be let go to waste. There's no point in him eating again at home. He'll just get fat. Eating two meals is sheer gluttony – a sin – and just fair eating money."

Both children burst out laughing and very promptly sobered when Elspeth glowered at them.

"Come, Mr Graham, say goodbye to the bairns and let's be off."

# Chapter 38

Eternally grateful still to be in the land of the living and not having been sucked further into that beckoning, brilliant white tunnel beyond whose white door, at the height of her illness, she had often glimpsed friends and relatives who had already passed into the land of the Leal, Becky decided her time just hadn't come. She faced most days with courage, cheerfulness, and an iron will to make the best of what life still had to offer her. Even so, there were still black days, no matter how desperately she tried to look on the bright side and count her blessings. But on those days, no matter how she prayed, communed with God, and even tried to exercise the right hand that she now referred to as her 'gammy hand', the hand refused to budge into any semblance of useful and meaningful life.

Her face awash with tears of frustration Becky would berate herself and yet again remind herself just how lucky she was even to be alive. Despite her bitter tears and regret for what was gone, ever so slowly, day by day, Becky was learning to cope with her new situation. Gradually she taught herself to write with her left hand even if the result was a horrific scrawl.

Then came the day of celebration: after much trial and error, false starts, and many muttered curses Becky actually managed to sew on a button! No apprentice seamstress was ever prouder of her work than was Becky of the somewhat askew button she had managed to affix to Val's blouse.

*Yes,* thought Becky, *suddenly life is taking on a much rosier hue.*

On the Friday evening of the week of her sewing triumph Becky sat relaxing with a cup of tea, listening to the wireless. The children were in bed and Ewan was working late. A rat-a-tat on her letter box brought her to her feet and downstairs to the entry hall. Pulling the door open to admonish the neighbourhood children she suspected of rattling her letter box, she was surprised to see a rather dishevelled Uncle Jack, looking totally unlike his normal, tidy, reserved, bank manager self.

"Becky," he blurted out, "the sick line's out for Meg at the Royal."

"But I saw her only last week – a bit frail and tired for sure, but fine."

"Becky, lass, you know as well as I do there's only one reason they send out the line at any hospital to let visitors in at any time."

With that Uncle Jack broke down sobbing and sagged against the door frame.

Becky knew exactly what was on his mind. The 'sick line' only went out when the hospital staff was fairly certain the patient was at death's door and the bed had been moved from the centre of the ward to the position closest to the entrance to make it easier to move the body to the morgue without upsetting the other patients.

Grabbing hold of Uncle Jack's arm, Becky tried to help him up the stairs. Fortunately, the neighbour next door saw what was happening and came to Becky's assistance. Between them they got Uncle Jack upstairs and seated in the living room. Anna, the neighbour, a great believer in the healing power of tea, bustled around Becky's kitchen getting them all hot sweet drinks.

As soon as Anna had heard Uncle Jack's story she insisted: "Becky, you and your uncle should get over to the Royal right away. I'll stay here and listen out for the children until such time as their daddy gets home from work. It'll be no bother to me,

Becky. Since Peter died and my two lads went off to the army, I'm glad of something to occupy my time."

As Anna saw them off she called after them: "Maybe she'll have taken a turn for the better by the time you get there. After all, where there's life there's hope."

With these words ringing in their ears, Becky and Uncle Jack set off for the nearest tram stop on the first stage of their journey across Glasgow to the massive Gothic structure of the Royal Infirmary.

# Chapter 39

For what seemed like an eternity, Becky and Uncle Jack had been sitting on either side of Meg's hospital bed. From time to time Meg would toss her head from side to side on the pillow and mutter incoherently. Each time this happened Becky would yet again place her hand on the old woman's arm in the rather forlorn hope that such human contact would in some way offer at least a modicum of comfort to the patient.

Meg's bed, which was nearest to the door, was shielded by screens, which although cutting out the sights of the ward did not exclude the myriad sounds and pungent hospital smells of the busy, overcrowded surgical ward. At one point when it looked as if Uncle Jack was on the point of collapse with the stress of their situation Becky suggested he should take a short break from their vigil.

"At least pop out for a puff or two of your pipe, Uncle Jack. Why don't you do that?"

At first the look on his face made it clear he would welcome such a respite, then instead he started a whispered conversation across the bed.

"You know, all this came on her suddenly. Mind you, now that I come to think of it, ever since your accident to your hand she hasn't been what you would call really well. Her sister, Nellie, dying while you were ill did upset her although in later years they weren't all that close right up till Nellie had that stroke last year. When you had that Tetanus she worried herself stupid about you.

You'll remember, able for the journey or not, she struggled every day from our place on Parliamentary Road to visit you in the Western Infirmary."

Becky had but a very hazy memory of her stay in hospital and no recall whatever of who had kept watch by her bedside at the height of her illness. She could only nod feebly as tried to choke back the tears which threatened to engulf her.

"Yes, loved you like a daughter she did. As if you were her very own daughter."

At these words Becky blinked in surprise. Almost as if the emotive words had struck a chord of some sort in the patient's befuddled brain, Meg without any warning became even more restless and distraught. Seeing this and worried that the overwrought, morphine-doped woman might inadvertently blurt out her lifelong secret and further upset her husband, Becky again pleaded with him to take a short break.

No sooner had Uncle Jack left than Meg roused into some semblance of her former mentally alert self.

*Perhaps she's going to get better after all,* Becky thought in a burst of optimism.

Becky looked down in amazement as she saw Meg's face clear. Then Meg grasped Becky's hand and in a clear voice said: "Becky! You are just my own lovely daughter, aren't you? My own darling wee girl … my daughter."

Meg's head fell back on the pillow. Her secret was at last out.

When Jack returned he was distraught, not only at the death of the woman he had loved for forty-plus years, but also with the regret of having missed her last minutes of lucidity.

After wiping his eyes and blowing his nose Uncle Jack stared hard at Becky.

"Meg's last words, you must tell me, Becky … did they concern me?"

Not wishing to lie to him, but at the same time having no desire to hurt him Becky thought: *My God. How can I possible tell him what she said? What her actual crystal-clear words were? How can I inflict on him the bitter knowledge that* his *name was not on her lips at the end?*

Uncle Jack's voice broke into her thoughts: "It's all right, Becky, don't torture yourself with indecision. I can see from your face. The expression tells it all ... Meg's last words had no meaning for *me*, so ..."

He fixed a steely gaze on Becky then in a voice deep with authority said: "Whatever she said to you on her deathbed was strictly between you, Meg and her Maker. I have no right, in fact no need, to know her last words. Nor does anyone else. They are a sacred trust for you, and that's the way they must always remain ... do you fully understand?"

Some time later as they left the infirmary arm in arm and stood in the pouring rain at the nearest tram stop, Uncle Jack turned to Becky and said: "One last thing I must say, Becky, and then I'll never again speak another word on the subject ... your Aunt Meg, God rest her soul, loved you like a *daughter*. You must always remember that. She loved you like the daughter she *never* had. We never had children of our own. The doctors said some accident, perhaps in her teens, had left her unable to have children, made her more susceptible than others to 'women's problems' so she never was all that robust."

Standing in the light of the street lamps with the rain dripping off her nose, Becky realised in a blinding flash that Uncle Jack, outwardly unemotional canny Scotsman that he was, had obviously known all along of Meg's guilty secret. She now knew it had been a measure of his love for Meg that throughout the years of their marriage he had gone along with the pretence, the massive lie, thus allowing her to maintain her dignity, her place in society, and finally take her secret to the grave.

# Chapter 40

Since Fairfields and all the other Clyde shipyards were engaged in essential war work, in order to keep the workforce well fed, the female employees at workmen's restaurants like Alex's were considered exempt from being called up to work in munitions or in an aircraft factory. That however, didn't mean that they couldn't volunteer for such well-paid work.

In the spring of 1943, a year after Becky's accident, Alex the owner of the Workman's Restaurant was at his wit's end. Ruby, the maid-of-all-work had left his employment without as much as a week's notice, giving as her explanation: "Ah can get good wages in the munitions factory. So Ah'm no working for peanuts ony mair. That's the last ashet pie or mince and tatties Ah'll serve."

Alex explained to Becky: "The yards are working full belt and all sorts of shift work. Ewan and I are run off our feet without an extra pair of hands particularly at the dinner hour. Would you consider coming in, say from about eleven until half after two or maybe three?"

Becky hesitated and looked self-consciously at her crippled hand.

Ewan said: "Don't worry about your hand, Becky. You've learnt to do most things with your left hand as if you'd been born left-handed. You manage everything about the house no bother. Come on, help us out. Give it a try. If you find it too much after the first couple of weeks, then Alex and I will just have to find someone else."

"Well, I suppose I could give it a go. With those hours I could be there when Val and Scott get home from school. I wouldn't want them coming back to an empty house."

She grinned at Alex. "And, of course, Val and Scott can have dinner here at mid-day, can't they … for free."

So Becky found herself installed as kitchen skivvy come front-of-house waitress.

At the end of her first week Alex said: "You've settled in very well, Becky. The shipyard workers like your cheery manner and the shopkeeper crowd that comes in after them also think you're great. Next thing you know you'll be getting a medal from the King for your war effort."

Becky laughed. "I don't know about that, but I must admit I'm quite enjoying the work and the repartee with the customers. It's nice to be out of the house for a spell and seeing people."

By mid-December of 1943 Becky was a well established fixture in the restaurant and had settled into a satisfactory routine for her household chores. Scott now twelve had sat and passed the all important Qualifying Exam – the dreaded Quallie – and had been informed that in January he would move from Greenfield School to the academic stream at Govan High School – PB1; Preparatory Boy's 1 – and in September of 1944 into First Year Secondary. Becky had, of course, informed Uncle Jack and Grampa Graham and both had accepted her invitation to a family tea to celebrate the news.

Becky baked a cream sponge for after the high tea having scoured the shops for anything fancier and found nothing in the virtually empty bakery stores.

When she produced the cake Uncle Jack laughed. "Trust you, Becky. Meg never could get the hang of baking with powdered eggs. Her cakes after rationing never really came out right. And here's you fed all of us a splendid meal of Spam fritters and home-made chips and topping it off with this fine looking cake."

The cake consumed down to the last bite they sat round the fireplace and Grampa Graham said: "You're a right clever wee lad, Scott. Before we know it you'll be spouting geometry theorems at us and speaking French like a native – maybe German or Latin too depending on which you take in Second Year."

Scott beamed at being the centre of attention and Becky stole a quick glance at Val.

*Val's in Third Year now, into Fourth in September*, Becky thought. *I hope this praise for Scott doesn't get her all jealous again. The bit about German or Latin is bound to irk her since she didn't get to take a second language.*

The gifts from Uncle Jack and Grampa Graham didn't lessen Becky's fears as a dictionary and geometry set were produced like rabbits out of a hat. However, to Becky's relief Val seemed quite unconcerned.

Uncle Jack and Grampa Graham gone, Becky turned to Ewan. "Well, that was very pleasant, Wasn't it? What a relief that Scott has passed the Quallie so well. We can be really proud of him, can't we?"

Ewan nodded. "Oh, yes. Marvellous, just great."

His tone of voice did not match the words spoken and Becky took a closer look at her husband in the light of the doorway.

"Don't get me wrong. I'm proud enough of Scott and of Val too for that matter. It's myself I'm not feeling quite so good about … in fact, there's something I have to tell you …"

# Chapter 41

It was with a sinking feeling of déjà-vu that Becky followed her husband back up the stairs. At once her mind filled with images of the never-to-be-forgotten time, also after a pleasant family get-together, when Ewan had confessed that he like thousands of others had been cast onto the scrap heap of unemployment.

*It couldn't be that again. Not now in the middle of the war. Had Ewan been called up after all – despite his age of forty-eight? No, that wasn't possible. Had he been conscripted for essential war work? He was, after all, a draughtsman even if he hadn't put pen to paper that way since 1936.*

"Becky, are you listening to me?" Ewan's voice broke into her thoughts.

"Oh, yes, of course ..."

"Of course, nothing, you were away with the fairies. You know Alex's wife passed away nearly two years ago? Well, now that Alex's pushing sixty, one of his sons, the one that lives in Dundee, wants him to sell up and go to live with his family. You've seen how breathless Alex gets when we're busy? It seems he has a heart condition of some sort and the doctor thinks it would be a good idea for him to go easier."

"So Alex is going to try to sell the restaurant?"

"Right. And you know what they say about new brooms. I'll be out on my ear. Mind you, the way things are now I should get a job of some kind no bother."

Ewan sighed. “It’ll be funny, after all these years, working anywhere else but the restaurant.”

“If Alex is determined to sell, why shouldn’t he sell the restaurant to you … or better still to us?”

Ewan looked at Becky as if she had taken leave of her senses. “Me … or us … buy a business? You really are away with the fairies aren’t you? Where would we get the money? We’ve done fine these last years, even managed to put a wee bit by for a rainy day, but buy the restaurant! Have you any idea how much it would cost? Alex’s not about to give it away for nothing.”

“I may not be as daft as you think,” Becky said, rising. “Wait here. Don’t move. I’ll be back in a minute.”

When Becky re-entered the living room she carried a large framed picture of a Highland stag, which had hung over the fireplace in their bedroom ever since the death of Aunt Meg.

“I know you hate this picture, Ewan …”

Ewan nodded and gave a sheepish grin. “You’re right there. It’s an awful picture. If it hadn’t come to you from your Aunt Meg the damned thing would have been in the dustbin not minutes after it arrived here.”

“Just forget all that for the moment. Undo the wee metal clips at the back.”

More to humour Becky than for any other reason, Ewan did as he was told. When the backing was removed a more glorious vista than any Highland stag at bay met their view.

Speechless for a moment Ewan gazed at the sight, his eyes wide in amazement and disbelief.

“What in God’s name?” he finally said. “I don’t understand. There must be hundreds of pounds here. Why would Meg leave *you* hundreds of pounds in tissue-paper five pound notes? Surely this should have gone to Uncle Jack? Why would she leave it to you? It isn’t even as if you were her daughter.”

Studiously ignoring the vexed question as to why she should have been entitled to the money, Becky said: “Isn’t it enough that Aunt Meg wanted me to have the money? Before her last illness she told me she had been putting aside money for years that she meant me to have, to give me and mine a good start in life."

"In cash? With Uncle Jack a banker? Shouldn't it have been in the bank?"

"She said she and Uncle Jack were well enough off. He never missed the money she saved from her housekeeping and anyway he would have a good pension from the bank when he retired, so they wouldn't need the money she had saved secretly."

"Why put it in the back of that hideous picture? Damn it, Becky, you might have tossed it out never knowing what was there."

"You're wrong there. She told me where she was hiding it and that Uncle Jack knew the picture was to go to me when she died."

"So you've known all along we had that money?"

"Yes, as you said we were doing okay – even saving a little. I was keeping it for a rainy day."

They removed the money and started counting.

"Becky, there's more than enough to buy the restaurant. I know what Alex wants."

"Good. I already know the routine, so there's no problem there. We can hire another girl or two and run the restaurant ourselves. That's settled. First thing tomorrow morning, don't waste a minute, get right down to business with Alex. Talk it over with him. I'm sure everything will be just fine."

Ewan hugged Becky. "It was a lucky day for me when I met you at Caz's wedding in Bridgeton."

Recalling how appallingly rude she had been to him on their first meeting, Becky was glad the passage of time had mellowed the memory.

# Epilogue

***September 1949***

The war years had been good to Becky and Ewan Graham. Apart from the evacuation upset right at the beginning and the odd broken window, they and their children had been spared the heartache and the utter horror which had blighted so many lives in different countries over the course of the conflict. In some ways the war had actually been good for them as the busy shipyards kept their restaurant – now named Graham's – packed with hungry workmen and queued out every dinner hour at the carry-out counter.

Ewan sighed. "I had thought the children would follow us into the business. I could see us ending up with a chain of restaurants like Miss Cranston's Tearooms ..."

"We can't live their lives for them, Ewan," Becky said. "Val's the teacher I never became. Scott's got a place at the university to study engineering. We've done well by them. It's up to them now to make their own way."

**The End**

## Also by Jenny Telfer Chaplin

### The Kinnons of Candleriggs

**An uncompromising story of one woman's life in Victorian Glasgow.**

Kate, a chamber maid, pregnant and unexpectedly married to the son of Irish landed gentry, expects a life fitting her husband's status, but her husband is cut off without a penny by his family. So, instead, as poverty-stricken Irish immigrants considered the lowest of the low by the Glaswegians, she has to battle religious, cultural, and social prejudice.

Told with humour, compassion, and a keen insight into the period, this is a first rate read.

**ISBN 1-904492-64-9**

**Also by Jenny Telfer Chaplin**

**The Widow of Candleriggs**

Kate Kinnon – the Widow of Candleriggs – having buried her domineering husband, is left struggling to support herself, her daughter, and granddaughter in 1901 Glasgow.

With her usual dogged determination, Kate overcomes the many setbacks and sees her daughter Jenny established in her own home with a loving husband.

Told with the same wry humour and compassion as her debut novel "The Kinnons of Candleriggs", Jenny Telfer Chaplin again shows keen insight into the period and provides a mesmerising, multi-faceted read.

**ISBN 1-905202-22-9**

www.bewrite.net

## Also by Jenny Telfer Chaplin

### The Ashes of Candleriggs

Kate Kinnon – The Widow of Candleriggs – having survived years of hardship and deprivation finds that Fate isn't finished with her yet, despite her new life of comparative luxury in Ireland.

However, Kate, ever the fighter, confronts and finally faces down problems which threaten to overwhelm her in this satisfying conclusion to the 'Candleriggs' Trilogy and the saga of the redoubtable Kate Kinnon.

**ISBN 1-905202-48-2**

www.bewrite.net

Printed in the United Kingdom
by Lightning Source UK Ltd.
134800UK00001B/28-66/P

9 781905 202584